D0341637

MAX QUIGLEY

Technically *NOT* a Bully

MAX QUIGLEY

Technically *NOT* a Bully

Written and Illustrated by
James Roy

Houghton Mifflin Books for Children
Houghton Mifflin Harcourt
Boston • New York • 2009

www.hmhbooks.com

Houghton Mifflin Books for Children is an imprint of
Houghton Mifflin Harcourt Publishing Company.

The text of this book is set in Guardi.

Library of Congress Cataloging-in-Publication Data
Roy, James, 1968–
Max Quigley : technically not a bully / written and illustrated by James
Roy. — 1st American ed.
p. cm.
Originally published: Australia : Puffin Australia, 2007.
Summary: After playing a prank on one of his "geeky" classmates,
sixth-grader Max Quigley's punishment is to be tutored by him.
ISBN 978-0-547-15263-9
[1. Tutors and tutoring—Fiction. 2. Bullies—Fiction. 3.
Friendship—Fiction.] I. Title.

PZ7.R81215Max 2009
[Fic]—dc22
2008036110

Manufactured in the United States of America
MP   10 9 8 7 6 5 4 3 2 1

For Bailey.

A truly beamish boy.

1 SKIN TAGS

That Monday I went to school, I had a meat pie for lunch, and it was nice.

Really, I should say that my pie *would* have been nice if that complete idiot Josh Hargreaves hadn't knocked it out of my hands and onto the ground. He claimed he was just trying to defend himself, but who defends himself with a pie? I mean, honestly! No one, that's who. And even worse, who defends himself with *someone else's* pie? That idiot Josh Hargreaves, that's who. Which just proves what an idiot he actually is.

So yes, my pie *would have been* nice, if I'd been able to eat more than two bites before stupid Hargreaves went and lashed out wildly after I flicked his ear, and knocked my half-eaten pie all over the ground. So I figured I was totally justified in throwing his baked bean sandwich onto the ground next to my tragically splattered pie and grinding it into the concrete with my shoe.

Mrs. Hinston didn't see it that way, but she's practically blind, so what would she know? Not much, since I told her halfway through detention that my irritable bowel syndrome was playing up and that I had to rush to the bathroom to avoid a very messy accident. She said I could go so long as I came straight back. I went, but I didn't go back.

On the way to meet Jared down near the tennis courts as planned, I ran into Triffin Nordstrom. Or Nerdstrom to his friends. If he had any. Which he doesn't, probably partly because of his faintly ridiculous first name, and partly because he's got no interesting aspects to his personality at all. Nerdstrom was sitting on one of the benches near the cricket nets, reading some absurdly fat book, and as I went past I caught him glancing up at me. I wondered if he was about to say something, but then he didn't, probably because he couldn't think of the right words to use. Elvish ones, for example.

I didn't care, though. Nerdstrom means nothing to me. He's like a boil on the bum of our school. Actually, that's not quite right, because a boil is irritating and weepy, like Luke Keynes in fifth grade.

Nerdstrom's more like a little skin tag, one of those little fatty nodules like the ones my grandma had just below her ear. Not painful, not really in the way, just there. Only noticeable at all if you know it's there and you bother to look.

Yeah, that's what Nerdstrom is. He's a skin tag.

2 A WORTHY ADVERSARY

That Tuesday I went to school, I had a pie for lunch, and it *would* have been nice if I hadn't thrown it against the library window trying to scare some of the first graders who were inside pulling stupid first grade faces at me and Jared. Kids these days have no respect. I've heard Dad say that, and I reckon he's right. When I was in first grade I never would have made faces at someone who'll be in seventh grade next year, or anyone older than me at all, for that matter.

And I decided something else that Tuesday. I decided that Mrs. Hinston holds a grudge. She *did* notice that I didn't come back from "going to the bathroom" the day before, so she added all of Monday's "incomplete" detention for flattening Josh Hargreaves's sandwich onto the detention for the Meat Pie Meets Window incident, and decided that that added up to three days of lunchtime detention, starting the following week. I'm glad I wasn't in her class in fourth grade, if that's an example of her math. Those poor kids wouldn't have a clue about addition or times tables or anything, if she thinks that one plus one is three.

She also said that Mum and Dad were going to get a note sent home the next time I did something "antisocial." Ordinarily I wouldn't have worried about that kind of threat, since teachers don't usually remember those things. But Mrs. Hinston had shown herself to be a Worthy Adversary, so I figured I was going to have to be careful.

3 MIRACLES OF MATH

That Wednesday I went to school and had a meat pie for lunch, and it *would* have been nice if I hadn't found a hair in it. I took it back to the canteen and told the lady, and even showed her the hair, and I said that I wanted my money back, or at the very least a new pie.

She looked at the hair and shook her head. She reckoned that it was one of my hairs, and said if she gave me my money back, all I'd do is spend it on candy and junk.

So I said, "Fine, just give me another pie."

But she said that after I'd eaten two-thirds of the pie I could tell that I would still be hungry when I'd finished, so I'd stuck a hair in it and took it back so I could get a whole new pie, which would add up to one and two-thirds of a pie for the price of one.

I said that her math was good, much better than Mrs. Hinston's, but that she was still wrong. Then I said, "Anyway, if that's true, how come I only eat one pie every other day, but I want one and two-thirds today?"

"I wouldn't know how many pies you have every day, lovey, but it certainly wouldn't surprise me if you *did* eat two pies for lunch every day," she said.

That was when I said, "We're lucky to get any pies at all when *you're* in the canteen."

And that's when she went mad, and called one of the teachers over, and told him that I'd called her fat. Which I hadn't, even though I could have, because she was.

And Mrs. Hinston went on to demonstrate yet another miracle of math by somehow making one plus one plus one equal five.

I decided then that on Thursday I'd have a sausage roll.

4 A RHETORICAL QUESTION, AND NERDSTROM DOESN'T THROW UP

That Thursday I went to school and had a sausage roll for lunch, and it was nice. It would have been nicer if I'd been able to eat it without interruption from several teachers, who were all wondering what I'd been up to, just because I was sitting quietly eating my lunch. One of them, Mr. Goward, was walking past on his way back from the canteen, and he said, "You're trouble, Quigley," and he was all sneery and mean, but I didn't say anything back to him, even when he added, "You've been up to something, haven't you?"

I said (quite respectfully, I thought), "No sir, I haven't."

But he just kind of sneered and said, "That was a rhetorical question, Quigley. Do you know what that is? It's a question that doesn't require an answer."

So I didn't say anything else, because his forehead veins were starting to bulge, and I already had five days of detention planned for the next week, and I didn't want to add to them. The way Mrs. Hinston's math had been going, one more detention was going to turn five lunchtimes into every single lunchtime until the end of the term, plus the possibility of some afterschool detention.

Besides, we were going on an excursion to a cake factory on Friday, and Mr. Sigsworth had grabbed me before lunch and told me that if he heard one more peep out of me I'd be staying behind and helping Ms. Lalor cover textbooks in the library. Which I've done before. That's how I knew it was a fairly useful threat. And it was also why I'd been trying very, very, *very* hard to be good. *Especially* good, as Mum would say. Which is weird, because I don't think you can be slightly good or very good. I've always thought you're either good or you're not, and if you go past being good and try too hard to be even better, you just end up being a suck-up. Which might look like being good to most adults, but to anyone with any intelligence, it looks like what it is. Sucking up. Which isn't good at all.

So I'd been trying hard to be good. Just *plain* good. See, if I'd been trying too hard, I would have jumped up from my seat, run after Mr. Goward and said,

"Please, Mr. Goward, sir, can I help you by cleaning up the playground today? It's really messy, and inconsiderate kids have been chucking their papers all over the ground, and it needs cleaning up." But then he would have just frowned sideways at me and told me that he *definitely* knew I was up to something then. So I decided that the best thing to do was to just sit quietly, say nothing, and let the teachers *believe* that I'd been doing something bad, when I actually hadn't.

Something else happened that Thursday apart from the sausage roll for lunch and my pretty impressive effort at being good. I was waiting in one of the lunch lines, and Nerdstrom was waiting in the one next to me, and I saw him peek my way. So I said, "What are you staring at, Nerdstrom?"

And he looked away, and I heard him say, "Nothing." Then he must have decided to get all brave or something, because he said, really quietly, "I'm not frightened of you."

"What was that?" I asked him.

And even though he looked like he was about to fall over from being too pale, he said it again. He said, "I just want you to know that I'm not frightened of you." Which was plainly wrong, because as I mentioned, he'd gone all pale in the head, and looked like he might even throw up, which would have been heaps funny. Smelly and messy, but still funny.

But he didn't throw up, and I said to him, "Why would you even tell me that you're not scared of me?"

That was when he said, "Because I'm not."

So I went, "Boo!" and sort of stamped my foot toward him, and he flinched like I'd slapped him across the face or something.

He is such a lamo weirdo.

5 A NON-RHETORICAL QUESTION

That Friday we went to a cake factory, I ate too many cheesecakes, and then I threw up on the bus. And I bet that Nerdstrom would have laughed at me along with everyone else if he hadn't been still back at the factory trying to get back into the factory shop through the emergency exit.

Places like cheesecake and chocolate factories that have schoolkids coming through all the time should have plans in place to make sure that those schoolkids don't eat too many of the free samples, and that they don't double-back to the end of the line for another free sample. Several times. And if each person is allowed only one piece of each sample, they should put out only as many pieces as there are people. It makes sense. Otherwise it's just encouraging kids to take more than one piece, then double-back, like I said.

So I was already feeling sick when we got to the factory shop, which is this place where they sell pies and cakes and puddings and things that still taste the same as the ones you buy at the supermarket, except the label's been put on the package crooked, or the pie's smaller than it's supposed to be, or too big sometimes, or the packet says "Apricot Danish" when it's actually a blueberry danish. And everything's heaps cheaper. It's the kind of place where poor people buy posh food.

So anyway, Mum was planning for some ladies to come over for this party where she shows them all these face creams and stuff, and they all put on perfume and tell each other how fabulous they smell, so she gave me ten dollars and asked me to get as many cheesecakes as I could, which ended up being five. But once we got on the bus, I had to check that I'd bought what I thought I was buying, so I opened one of the boxes. And it was what I'd thought it was, which was good, but I couldn't really give it to my mum opened, so me and Jared ate it, even though after all the free samples I'd eaten I wasn't really hungry at all, and was actually feeling sick.

Then we thought we'd better check another one of the boxes, and we ate that cheesecake as well, just to make sure that it was only in the factory shop because it was slightly out of shape, and not because they'd put salt in it instead of sugar, which can happen, since salt and sugar look almost exactly the same anyway. But they'd done that one right, because it was really, *really* sweet, and not at all salty.

Then we opened another one, and I was feeling *heaps* sick by then, so rather than actually eating it, I just flicked bits of it at some of the girls, who were going to tell on us until me and Jared threatened to get them when we got back to school. So they just cried instead. Girls are so stupid, the way they cry so easily.

By the time we were down to our last cheesecake, we were feeling so sick, but I couldn't really go home and tell Mum that we could get only one cake for ten dollars, so we decided to get rid of it. By eating it. That was when I threw up. It was a heaps big spew, that's for sure, right in the aisle of the bus, and you could even see bits of blueberry in some of it, and everyone was squealing and going on about how gross it was, and all the girls that we'd made cry were laughing now, which made me pretty angry. I mean, haven't they ever felt that sick? If they had, they'd know how awful it is to just feel that really uncomfortable hotness and coldness, and your throat's all tight, and your stomach sort of bounces up and down, and how it tastes all different coming up, and bits go up the back of your nose, which stings a lot. Jared told the other kids to shut up and stop laughing, and so did Mrs. Hale, but it didn't stop them. In fact, one of the girls still had a blob of cheesecake on her cheek from when we'd flicked it at her, and Mrs. Hale thought that I'd thrown up so violently that I'd got her from several seats away. *That* was funny, especially when she started gagging as well. Mrs. Hale, that is.

But the funniest thing of all was when we got back to school. Nerdstrom's mum was there, and we watched her waiting patiently as the kids filed off the bus. Then she came up to Mr. Sigsworth and asked where Triffin was, and he said that he'd been told that she was picking him up early at the factory for his violin lessons. The story was complete bull. That was just what we'd told the teachers when we all got on the bus at the end of the tour and they did a head count and asked why there was one less than there should have been. When Mr. Sigsworth had found out that Nerdstrom's mum had picked up Triffin without telling either of the teachers, he'd been heaps cross that he'd not been told earlier, but he'd told the bus driver to go anyway. Which was the funniest thing about the whole day, because Jared and I had pushed Nerdstrom out one of the exits in the factory shop, and there was a sign on the door that said THIS DOOR LOCKS FROM THE INSIDE. EMERGENCY EXIT ONLY.

But when Mrs. Hale made a call on her phone, and Nerdstrom's mum went and got into her crappy old orange Volvo and sped off, and Mr. Sigsworth started turning in circles going, "Where are Max Quigley and Jared Fernmarsh? Where the *blazes* are Quigley and Fernmarsh?" (which definitely wasn't a rhetorical question, judging by the confused look on his face), we knew that the joke was over. And we knew that even Mrs. Hinston's creative math wasn't going to explain how long we were about to be put in detention for.

6 CRIME AND PUNISHMENT

I'd really done it this time. Man, were Mum and Dad peed off about the whole Nerdstrom thing! Not that it was *all* our fault. Nerdstrom had been pretty annoying all day, especially when he tried to tell Mr. Sigsworth that me and Jared were going back for extra free samples. We saw him do it, and that really irritates me, when kids tattle. The way I see it, if a teacher isn't good enough at their job to see what's going on around them, they should either find another job where they can see everything they need to see without even trying that hard (like standing in one of those freeway tollbooths, for example) or just accept that stuff is going to happen. Stuff like kids getting pushed out of emergency exits and left there to find their way around the back of the factory, through a warehouse and between about a gazillion trucks and forklifts.

Mum and Dad were pretty much in total agreement with all the people at school, which I suppose is predictable. They always take the teachers' side. Always. I can't think of a single time when they disagreed with a teacher.

Actually, there was one time, back in fourth grade, when Ms. Gleeman said that I'd done a heaps good job on my project about India, and my parents disagreed. She tried to argue, until they pulled out my brother Cameron's fourth grade project on India from two years before, the one where he got nine out of ten. They showed her how I'd just done a color photocopy of Cameron's project and put a new title page on it. So you see, even when they disagree with the teachers, they're taking someone else's side instead of mine.

So for the Cheesecake Caper, as me and Jared called it, I was given a pretty harsh range of punishments, considering that no one actually got hurt. They were as follows:

1. Grounded. Predictable, but pretty effective, I think. A standard kind of punishment, favored by parents of kids who go out a lot or play sports, especially kids of my age. I'll be in seventh grade next

year, although Mum says that it's "touch and go" as to whether I'll survive that long. Grounding doesn't really work for kids who have no friends or stay in a lot. For example, Nerdstrom would find being grounded a completely wasted experience. But I was missing out on several very important games of baseball, which was highly frustrating. So all in all, a good choice of punishment. It also meant that I couldn't see Jared. I decided that his parents and mine planned all this together.

2. No pocket money. Again, fairly standard. Most kids my age get between five and ten dollars a week, depending on how cheap their parents are. Mine are moderately cheap—they give me ten. That was going to hurt, although being grounded meant that there was nowhere to spend it anyway. I wasn't sure that they'd thought this one through so well. Oh yeah, except Mum said I had to buy five cheesecakes at full price out of my own money, which did kind of make it an okay punishment, I guess.

3. No TV, computer, or PlayStation. I knew this was going to seriously sting. But once again, they hadn't really done their homework, because I had a Gameboy Advance that they didn't know I had, which I bought off a second grade kid for two dollars, a can

of drink, and a broken Hotwheels launcher. It even came with ten games, eight of which were actually okay. Under the covers late at night, I knew they wouldn't have a clue.

4. No telephone. Hmm. Tough, but not the end of the world. Jared and I would still be able to see each other at school, especially in lunchtime detention, which was a separate but related form of punishment devised by the school independently of my parents.

5. Dishes every night. Stupid punishment, when

Punishment #5

← me

plate

perfectly good dishwasher (waste of money)

tea towel

you considered that we had a perfectly good dishwasher tucked under the kitchen bench. And yet this was how I would be expected to use my empty and TV-free evenings for the next month.

Dumb, dumb, dumb.

7 DAD UPS THE ANTE

Then, that Sunday, without any warning, and just as I thought that I had my head around the punishments devised by my sadistic parents, they figured right out of the blue that all the previously listed punishments were still not enough. They decided to "up the ante," as Dad calls it. He said that six years of being a bully was enough, and I'd have agreed with him, except technically I'm not actually a bully. Bullies wait behind lunch sheds and steal kids' Twinkies. I've never stolen anything in my life. Bullies beat people up. I've never actually punched anyone in my entire life, unless you count Jared, and that was just because he leaned forward as I *pretended* to swing at him, and I accidentally knocked him down and split his lip. That was different. Just like all those times I got into fights with Cameron. He's my brother, and that doesn't count.

The other things bullies do is hurt people. And I

don't mean just a flick on the ear or a punch to the leg. I mean *hurt* people, hurt them until they cry or have to go to the hospital. And as far as I know I've never caused anyone to get taken to the hospital. Or cry. Except for my brother, but we've been over that.

I've never even made Nerdstrom cry, and he's about the cryingest-looking person I've ever seen. He always seems like he's about to burst into tears, especially when he has to present to the class. He's got a heaps quiet voice anyway, but once he has to stand up in front of people and talk, his face goes pale, like he's going to pass out, then it goes red, and he mumbles whatever he has to say and scurries back to his seat as soon as he's finished, sometimes even before he's finished.

Anyway, even though I've never made anyone cry, Dad reckoned that I was in fact a bully, and that being grounded and not having access to the computer or the telephone and not having any pocket money and having to wash about a gazillion dishes every night was not enough of a punishment. Which is why that Sunday we went over to Nerdstrom's house. By *we* I mean Mum, Dad, and me, while Cameron got to stay home playing PlayStation with his annoying mate Adam. I wasn't at all happy about this, but I decided that with the level of punishment now being handed out I wasn't really in a position to disagree.

On the way out there, Mum and Dad made me practice what I was going to say, which felt very strange, apologizing to no one at all. But I did it.

Nerdstrom and his mum live in a pretty wacko house. It's kind of out in the bush, which isn't that far from town, really. We've got bushland everywhere near us, and I've heard that some weirdos like to go bushwalking, which seems to me to be an odd thing to do, since the bush is really just dust and rocks and crooked trees and sharp grass and pokey sticks. But some people like it, out there in the bush. Weird people, like I said.

Weird people like Nerdstrom and his mum, who live out along this rough dirt road, and there are all these birds that chatter and carry on constantly. If it wasn't for the birds making all that racket there'd be no sound at all except for all the wind chimes tinkling and clanging and stuff. To be completely honest all that noise would drive me completely crazy, but as we pulled up and got out, Mum said, "Wow, Steve, isn't this *gorgeous!*"

Dad went, "Mm-hm," which is kind of what he does when his mind is on other things. I think that on this occasion he was thinking about what he was going to say, which is pretty dumb, since going out there was his idea after all, and you'd think he'd get himself better prepared.

Anyway, we rang the doorbell, which was a cowbell hanging beside the big heavy door, and a minute later the door opened up and Nerdstrom's mum was standing there. Man, was *she* a surprise package! She was wearing really loose-fitting bright purple pants and this thing that looked like an old person's blanket with a hole in the top, which she'd stuck her head through. And she wasn't wearing any shoes at all, and she had rings on some of her toes. Plus there were her bright red glasses. And she said, in this really bizarre accent, "Hello. I'm Ulrika. I'm so glad you came."

Dad went, "Mm-hm," again, and Mum said, "It was a good idea. I think it will be good for the boys to talk about it." Which is when I suddenly understood that this wasn't Dad's idea after all, but Nerdstrom's mum's idea. And this made me heaps mad, right off. So I took a step backwards, but Dad put his arm around my back and pulled me forward a tiny bit, just enough so I knew that I had to stay, and that he was going to be there as well. Which made me feel a lot better about Dad, to be honest.

It was funny, though, how when I looked around at all that bush I started wondering how long I could live as an outlaw or a bushranger before I ran out of food.

Nerdstrom's mum took us into their house and said we could sit on their couch, which had these rugs and cushions all over it. I have to admit that it was quite a nice house, even though it was very small and smelled strange. It was heaps more colorful than our house, with rugs on the floor and pictures on the wooden walls and all that kind of stuff. Plus there were some weird statue-y kinds of things sitting around the place.

Mrs. Nordstrom asked us if we wanted tea, and my parents said yes please, and then she asked me if I'd like a juice or something, and I said okay. She got up and went into the kitchen, which was just off the room where we were, and while she was getting the drinks she called out to Nerdstrom, "Triffin, dear, our guests are here." When she called out, her accent was even stronger, especially the way she said Triffin. It was kind of like "*Tree*fern." And then I started to think that if we ever got into trouble for calling him Nerd-strom, we could start calling him Treefern instead. Which isn't quite as funny, but opens up a whole lot of different possibilities for jokes and things.

Then Mrs. Nordstrom stuck her head around the corner from the kitchen. "I hope chai tea is all right," she said, and Mum and Dad said yes, that was fine, even though I know for sure that Dad usually drinks only really strong black coffee or beer. Plus that muddy-looking stuff in a wooden bowl they gave him and Mum that time we went to Fiji for a holiday, but that was a special occasion, I guess.

A couple of minutes later she came back out with a tray, with cups and a teapot on it, as well as a couple of tall glasses full of really crazy-looking green juice.

Treefern
Nordstrom

"There you go, Max," she said, and she handed me one of the glasses. "I hope you like it. It's wheatgrass, celery, and dew-melon." Then she listed all these illnesses that I'll never get that that kind of awful juice is good for, like high blood pressure and tumors and nervousness. I must have made a face of some kind, though, because she laughed and said that it wasn't as bad as all that, and Dad gave me a pretty cranky look.

Then Nerdstrom came in. He looked heaps nervous, I have to say, which is understandable in one sense, but really dumb in another, since it was his house and his mum had just given me a large glass of evil juice that was probably going to kill me within minutes of taking my first sip anyway.

"Say hello to the Quigleys, dear," Nerdstrom's mum said, and Nerdstrom looked kind of pale and vomity again and said hello. And of course my parents were sickeningly sweet in reply, gushing on about how lucky he was to live in such a wonderful environment.

Then Mrs. Nordstrom said, "And say hello to Max, dear," and he looked at me and sort of coughed, then said, "Hi." So of course I said hi back, because that's polite.

"So I think we all need to talk about what happened on Friday," said Mrs. Nordstrom.

"Yeeees," said my mum.

Dad just nodded, and Nerdstrom blinked and looked at the floor, and I didn't know what to say or do, since it felt like everyone was looking at me, even though they actually weren't.

Then Mum said, "Max, do you have something to say to Triffin and his mum?"

So I said the stuff we'd practiced in the car. I said, "I'm sorry about what we did, and that you got left behind at the factory."

"And . . ." said my mum.

I said, "And what?"

"Was there anything else?"

"And I'm sorry that Mrs. Nordstrom had to go and pick him up from the factory."

Then Mum said, "To *her,* Max, not to me."

So I looked at Nerdstrom's mum and said, "I'm sorry that you had to go and pick up Nerd . . . Triffin from the factory, Mrs. Nordstrom."

"Please, call me Ulrika, and thank you for the apology."

"Remember what else we talked about?" Dad reminded me.

And I did remember, so I said, "I'm sorry that it made you worried."

Mrs. Nordstrom had taken off her mad red glasses and was wiping her eyes with a tissue. "Thank you, Max, it was very worrying indeed," she said. "I don't have anyone else in my life, you see, and Triffin is everything to me, so to think that something might have happened to him . . ."

"Can I say something now?" Nerdstrom asked, and his mum looked surprised. She sniffed and put her glasses back on.

"Of course, dear," she said.

Nerdstrom stood up and stared at me and said, "I don't know why you came here today." I could tell that he was pretty cross, from the way his nostrils were getting bigger and smaller, and his hands were all clenched up until his knuckles went white. I noticed that his wrists were really thin, too.

"Triffin! Max came here to apologize," his mum said, but Nerdstrom wasn't finished.

"I don't care if he says sorry a million times and buys me stuff and does anything else you can think of, because I know he doesn't mean it, and I know that when we get back to school on Monday it's not going to be the same."

His mum said, "That's right, dear, it's not."

But Nerdstrom *still* wasn't finished, and now his face was starting to go really red, as usual when there's an audience. "No, it's not going to be the same, Ulrika, because it's going to be worse, and I know you thought that making him come here into our house was the right thing to do, but it was the *stupidest* thing you could have done, because he'll be looking around here at all our stuff and he's going to just make fun of it and tell everyone what weirdos we are, because we are, and I hate you, Ulrika, and I hate you as well, Max, but I don't hate you two, Mr. and Mrs. Quigley, because I don't know you very well, but I don't think I like you very much, if *that* is the kind of son you made. And one more thing," he said then, looking at me. "I meant what I said the other day. I'm not afraid of you. I just don't like you, you . . . you *idiot jerk*."

And then he turned and walked out and slammed the door, and all the little beads that were hanging in the doorway all sort of jingled and rattled. Which is when I decided that he'd made a couple of good points in his little speech, and started looking around at all their things, making a mental list of crazy hippie stuff that I needed to tell Jared about.

Mrs. Nordstrom looked quite embarrassed, which I was pretty glad about, because her son had just proved what a troubled young man he was. Especially when you consider that we were good enough to go all the way out into the bush and beyond reach of all civilization to apologize for something that wasn't ever that big a deal in the first place.

I didn't say any of this in the car on the way home, though, because Mum and Dad weren't saying much, and I figured that it was a good idea just to lie low for a minute and say nothing.

When we got home, Dad turned off the engine in the driveway and turned around in his seat to face me. "So, what did you think of that?" he asked.

"What do you mean, what did I think?"

"Did you think that was a valuable thing to do?"

"No, not really," I replied.

"Why not?" Mum asked.

"Because all he did was tell us how much he hates us, and have this huge tantrum."

Then Dad said (to Mum, I think), "Uh-huh," which I think was his way of saying, "See?"

"What did *you* think?" I asked, but Mum just turned around and looked at me for a couple of really long seconds. At least, that's how it felt.

Then she said, "Maybe the way he reacted simply shows us how hurt he's been by all the horrible things you've done to him." Which is rubbish, I reckon. Like I said before, most of the things that have happened to Nerdstrom when I've been around have either been completely his own fault or just jokes that have gone a little bit wrong.

So that was Sunday. I wondered if Nerdstrom was going to be at school the next day. Probably.

Would I be nice to him? Of course.

Would I be taking back my apology, since it was met with such bad grace? I expected so.

Was he going to apologize for what he said to me, even though "idiot jerk" is a pretty odd kind of name to call someone? You betcha he was.

8 DOING TIME

That Monday I had a meat pie for lunch, and it was nice. Or at least, it would have been nice if I hadn't had to eat it in the detention room, which isn't some special room just for holding detention in, but the classroom of whichever teacher is supervising detention for that day. And that day the supervisor was Mrs. Beech, who is one of the second grade teachers. She has red hair and brown freckles and pale skin and always has a cold, which means she's constantly sneezing and blowing her nose. So not only is her hair red, but so are her eyes and the end of her nose.

I was pretty sure that Mrs. Beech didn't like me very much. She reckoned that she was ready for me that day. She looked up as I arrived at the door of the classroom and said, "Ah, Max Quigley. I've been expecting you."

"And I've been expecting to be here," I said, which made her frown and sneeze.

"Just sit down and say nothing. Did you bring your lunch?" I held up my pie and juice box. "And did you bring something to do?" I held up my wrestling magazine. "Try again," she said, and when I shrugged she sighed and handed me a math worksheet. "Now sit," she said, as if I were just a dog or something. I thought briefly about sitting on the floor right where I was, but I decided against it when I saw her red eyes get narrow and slitty.

There were three kids in detention, besides me. There was Mitchell Lackey, who is in fifth grade and likes to hurt birds and lizards and first graders and other small animals he manages to catch. He's seriously peculiar. Sitting behind him was Justin McElvoy. They're best friends. I guessed that they were there over the same incident, since they seem to do practically everything together. All the natural fauna within a square kilometer of the school were probably breathing a sigh of relief that those two were both in detention for the day.

The other kid there was Katie Hardcastle. She was almost certainly there because she'd been super-sassy to one of the teachers. I've met a few cheeky kids in my years at Church Street Public, but Katie Hardcastle would definitely have to be the worst. I've seen teachers argue with her for half an hour, just because it doesn't matter what they say to her, she has something to say in reply, every single time. She's fantastic like that. Once, in fourth grade, Mr. Clancy told her in front of the whole class that she had a serious problem with needing to have the last word.

"No I don't," she said.

Mr. Clancy blinked and said, "Actually, you do, Katie."

But she said, "I really don't."

"Fine, you don't then—just sit down."

"Well, maybe you're right, but I doubt it," she replied, and he started to get really cranky then.

"I'd like you to speak to your teachers with some respect, thank you."

"You're welcome," Katie said.

His voice was starting to get shaky now. "That's it, you're in detention!" he said.

But Katie replied, "No I'm not."

"Yes you are, young lady!"

"No I'm not. At lunchtime I will be, but right now I'm actually standing here on my chair arguing with you."

Then Mr. Clancy closed his eyes and scratched his forehead. When he opened his eyes he said,

"Get down off the chair, thank you."

Katie said, "I know you can't make me, because I know the rules, and if you touch me I'll scream, then my parents will sue you for assault."

And it went on like that for ages, until Mr. Clancy finally said, "Oh, I give up," and he did give up. But Katie didn't. She's tough. I think she could win a staring contest with

one of those fluffy hat guards that stand out in front of Buckingham Palace in London.

When I saw Katie in Mrs. Beech's classroom that Monday, I guessed that it was something similar that had led to her being in detention this time. People like Katie never do learn, I think that's true. And the thing is, I reckon that heaps of teachers don't even bother after a while. I think they just go, "If I can get through this year, this kid will soon be someone else's problem." Except we were only a week or two into the school year, and she was already in detention, which meant that her teacher still had a lot of year to get through before Katie became someone else's problem.

Detention was pretty boring. It always is. But I didn't really mind, because Jared was away from school that day, so all I would have been doing all lunchtime was wandering around by myself anyway.

Speaking of people being away from school, Nerdstrom wasn't there either that day. I figured he was probably just sulking like the big baby that he is.

9 NERDSTROM STAYS AWAY

That Tuesday I had a sandwich for lunch because the canteen was out of meat pies and sausage rolls. And the lady I'd had the fight about the hair in the pie with was there again, so that all made sense. And the sandwich was okay, I guess, but I would have preferred a pie. I saw a number of other kids with pies, and I thought about convincing one of them to swap their pie for my cheese sandwich, but I was already running late for my lunchtime detention, so I didn't.

Jared was at school, and of course he joined me in detention. He said that he'd had the beginnings of a cold the day before, but that he was feeling a lot better now. Obviously Nerdstrom wasn't over whatever it was he had, because he was still away. Either that or he was still sulking. What a jerk. What an idiot jerk.

It was probably just as well for Nerdstrom that he wasn't there, actually, because Mr. Sigsworth had an announcement to make. Just before recess he said to everyone, "All right, listen up. Our class has volunteered to do an assembly later in the term for our sixth grade Literature Day, and you're each going to do something."

One of the girls said, "But Book Week isn't until third term, is it?"

Mr. Sigsworth smiled and said, "That's true, but we thought that this year we'd have a Literature Day early in the year as well. We thought it was important for the younger kids to see that you older ones are into books and reading. It's a good example for them, you see? So I want you to do something, either on your own or in groups, to do with a favorite book. It can be a skit, or a poem, or a short play."

I put my hand up, and Mr. Sigsworth said, "Yes, Max?"

I said, "Can me and Jared do a performance? We could be wrestlers."

Mr. Sigsworth sighed and looked at the carpet. "Did you fall asleep during the words *Literature Day,* Max?" he said. "Generally that means that it has something to do with books."

"There are books about wrestling," I said.

"That you've actually read yourself, Max?" he asked, which I thought was unnecessary. "No, I'll be making sure that everything is aboveboard, and we don't have to decide now, but you might like to start thinking about what performance you or your group would like to do. But everyone needs to prepare something."

"Even Nerdstrom?" I called out. "Because he blushes really bad."

The class laughed, but Mr. Sigsworth shook his head. "Triffin's not even here to defend himself, Max. And yes, even he will have to do something for the assembly. Now get out of here, all of you. It's recess."

Me and Jared started talking about what we were going to do, and wrestling it was. It hardly even needed to be discussed, really. This was going to mean an unscheduled visit to the library, but we were determined to find a book about wrestling that would support our plan. Eventually.

Yep, we'd find a book with wrestling in it, and then I was going to be Robbie Bloodhound, and Jared could be Nemesis.

Yes, it really was quite an excellent plan.

10 **THE KID**

That Wednesday I had a pie for lunch, which I ate in detention. I also spilled some of it down the front of my shirt. The kid sitting next to me laughed, and I made a seriously threatening face at him. Then I almost felt bad, just for a second, because this kid was so tiny and weedy. He looked like he was in about first grade. I mean, I was in third grade before I got my first lunchtime detention, and this kid looked like he still needed a morning nap at recess time! I tried to think of what such a little kid would have to do to get lunchtime detention, but I couldn't imagine what. Wetting his pants in class, maybe. Either that or something totally unexpected and rather admirable.

But that didn't change the fact that he was actually laughing at me. I could hardly believe it, so I made another even more threatening face at him. He didn't seem too frightened by this either, and I had to admire his ability to remain calm even when confronted by someone like me.

"Don't you know who I *am?*" I asked him in a whisper.

The kid nodded and said, "Yeah, you're Max Quigley," as if I were stupid or something, and didn't know my own name.

So I said, "Yeah, so you should have more respect, since I'm heaps older than you, *and* because I could make your life here really unpleasant."

And that was when he shrugged and went back to drawing in his project book.

That made me really mad. Especially when I saw that what he was drawing in his project book was a

spiky green hair (which I don't have) →

← 3 fingers ??

apparently pie gravy is all squiggly ???

duck feet?

me, by some little kid I totally HATE

picture of someone with biggish ears, crooked teeth, and a big splat of pie down the front of his shirt. I mean, my ears aren't all that big. And I don't have green hair.

I decided then that I was *so* going to get him.

11 THE KID RETURNS

That Thursday I had nothing for lunch because I forgot to take my lunch money. On my way to the detention room, I was about to lean on a couple of the smaller kids hanging around the canteen to get some money out of them, but Mrs. Hinston (whose memory must be close to paranormal) spotted me and said, "Max Quigley, aren't you meant to be in Mr. Goward's classroom for detention today?"

"I don't have any lunch," I explained.

She looked at the little kids I was standing close to and said, "I don't think any of *them* brought your lunch to school, do you? Now hurry along to Mr. Goward's room, thank you." Which was very rude, since she actually asked me a question, but didn't even wait for the answer. Rhetorical questions can sometimes seem rude, I decided.

The little kid that drew a picture of me the day before was there again, and I thought I should sit near him, since he seemed to be getting too big for his boots. I mean, I wouldn't ordinarily sit that close to anyone younger than me, but I thought it would be wise to keep an eye on him. And when he saw me walk in, he just kind of nodded at me, all grown-up, and I just nodded back. I thought about making an intimidating face, but the way he looked at me I thought was actually pretty cool. Especially when you think that for a first grader to end up in lunchtime detention for two days in a row, *and* without crying as well, he must have done something pretty bad. They usually go fairly easy on the little ones, and just give them a paper pickup or something simple like that. But lunchtime detention for two days? In first grade? *That's* impressive.

I decided then that if he was there again the next day I was going to ask him what he'd done to deserve three days of detention.

12 A LITTLE CHAT WITH NERDSTROM

The first grade kid wasn't in detention that Friday, which disappointed me. But I knew I'd see him around, and I was going to make sure I asked him what he did to earn his detention. I mean, that's what I thought I'd do, except that I'd forgotten one important fact—that all little kids look practically the same. But at the time I did think that if I ever saw that kid again I was going to ask him what he'd done. It was sure to be pretty cool, whatever it was.

Nerdstrom was finally back at school. I saw him just after I arrived. I knew he was trying to act like I didn't frighten him, but I noticed that when he came around the corner from the library (where he was probably helping cover books or file newspapers or something) and saw me, he hesitated, just a little. Then he quickly kept walking, just so I would know that he wasn't scared of me. But I'm not stupid. I saw the tiny pause in his step, and the way he started blinking and looking at the floor a lot.

No, I'm not stupid.

And later, when I told Jared about it, he said that he thought it was time we had a talk to Nerdstrom, just one-on-one.

Or two-on-one, actually.

It went pretty well, considering. I think he saw our point of view. I mean, Jared was all for really scaring him, even hurting him, but like I said before, actually hurting people on purpose isn't my way. I don't want to let myself get labeled like that. Besides, I'm already on a lifetime of detentions as it is, so doing anything that leaves marks on the skin would be just plain stupid.

And of course if I was involved in hurting someone it would stuff up the balance of things. As it is, I can get people to see my point of view by talking to them. I persuade them. And sometimes I use Jared's pretty fearsome reputation as reinforcement for my persuasion. It's sort of like a good cop, bad cop kind of thing.

Anyway, this is how our talk with Nerdstrom went down. When we were getting our books and

good
cop
(me)

bad
cop
(Jared)

stuff out of our bags before morning assembly, I walked really close behind him and said, "We need to talk."

"Talk? About what?"

"We're not going to discuss it *here*," I said, and he just kind of swallowed. Or gulped, really, which is a scared kind of swallow.

So I said to him, "Don't stress about it, Nerdstrom. I just want to talk to you at recess time. I'll meet you down next to the Mud Pie Stump." There's this old sawn-off tree trunk beside the tennis courts where the little kids like to get all messy in the mud when the playground teachers aren't paying attention, which seems to be all the time for most kids and never at all when I'm around.

And when I said this, Nerdstrom went kind of pale, and he said, "I'm not frightened of you, Quigley," which was beginning to get annoying, to be honest, because I might have been starting to believe him. Even though his face was the color of this page and he looked fidgety, I was actually starting to think that I wasn't scaring him as much as I wanted to, or expected to.

So at recess I caught Nerdstrom's eye and sort of suggested to him that it was time for him to be moving down toward the stump.

When me and Jared got there, he was waiting for us, trying to look all relaxed but doing a really bad job of it. He saw us coming and jammed his hands right into his pockets like he was this cool guy and he said, "What's up?" Some people can say that and get away with it, but some people (like Nerdstrom) just sound stupid talking that way. I think he actually meant to say "Wassup" but said it wrong, like this American guy who visited our school once to talk about using less water when you shower, and instead of just saying "G'day" he said it as two words, like "Good day!" What a jerk.

So when Nerdstrom said, "What's up?" I said, "What's up is that I'm not happy with the way things are going around here. You're not playing the game."

"What game?"

"The game where you're scared of me."

"But I'm not," he said.

"Well you should be, because that's how things are around here. I'm the biggest kid in the school, and I don't want dumb little hippies like you getting too big for their boots. So I've already said I'm sorry for what happened at the cake factory place the other day, and now that I've done that, things should just go back to the way they've always been."

Nerdstrom coughed, cleared his throat, and said, "But . . . but even though you said you were sorry, I never accepted your apology. So . . . so it actually means nothing." Then his voice kind of trailed away.

"Why doesn't it mean anything?" I asked.

"Because you aren't really sorry."

Jared stepped in then and said, "How do you know that?"

"Because I heard you two laughing about it with some of the other guys yesterday, how you'd locked me out of the factory. And anyway, I don't really want your apology. I don't want anything from you."

"How about a black eye?" Jared asked him, as he took a step forward, which made Nerdstrom blink and wince. But it was strange how seeing him flinch didn't make me feel as good as it normally would have done.

Nerdstrom said, "I just want to be left alone, that's all. So can I go now?" And when we didn't say anything, he hopped down off the stump and walked off up the hill, looking back over his shoulder once or twice.

13 THE BIG, STUPID IDEA

There were some unfortunate developments that weekend. The main one of these concerned Nerd-strom, who now seemed intent on worming his way into every part of my life.

It began when Mum and Dad started talking about my math grades. I mean, it was early in the year, so grades shouldn't even mean that much. But they seemed to be on my case a lot earlier in sixth grade. Dad said all of my grades were suffering, but especially math. It's just like him to worry about things like math. Personally I don't really care about numbers very much, except for the obvious things, like how much a can of drink costs, or a new computer game, that sort of thing. You know, money stuff. Which is important, obviously. But what is all this equation stuff about? Mr. Sigsworth writes this big long list of numbers and things on the board, then he says, "Now I need you to work out the value of x in this equation."

But I think, Who cares?

It turns out that I have an ally in Katie Hardcastle. The other day Sigsy wrote out this long, complicated thing on the board and said, as usual, "Okay, class, what is x in this equation?"

Katie said, "What's x?"

"That's what I want you to work out, Katie."

To which she said, "But *what* is it? Is it eggs, or apples, or little piles of dog poo?" (That got a big laugh.)

Sigsy just shook his head and said, "It doesn't *matter* what it is, Katie."

So she put her pen down and said, "Good. Then we don't need to work it out, do we?"

Sometimes that girl makes so much sense.

Anyway, so my math grades were suffering, apparently. There'd been a note about it in my homework diary earlier in the week, sealed in an envelope. And on Saturday Mum and Dad called me into the kitchen and said, "Mr. Sigsworth is very worried about your application in class, especially in math." In reply, I named at least five other people who have much worse application in class, including Katie Hardcastle, and of course they said that those kids were the problem of *their* parents, not of mine, and that if Mr. Sigsworth thought it necessary to send a sealed letter home in first term outlining his concerns, then obviously they needed to do something about it. And since it is so very important to my parents that I be able to work out what x is at any given moment, they said they were going to get me some extra help. Imagine my surprise when I found out who it was going to be.

So I was like, "You're kidding! Nerdstrom? Why him?"

"Because he's good at math, that's why," Mum replied.

"How did you pick *him,* though? There are heaps of kids who are good at math, but *they* can actually talk to you without getting all nervous and looking like they're about to spew everywhere. Plus he's in my grade."

And that was when I saw Dad catch Mum's eye and raise his eyebrows, and he said, "It's final, all right, son? It's already been . . . you know, discussed. We've been talking to your teacher and some other people, and—"

"Do *I* get to discuss it?" I shouted, but of course Dad just shook his head.

"I'm sorry, mate. There's more to it than you realize."

"Well I think it's the stupidest idea anyone's ever had," I said, but Dad just glanced at Mum, then folded his arms.

"Yes, well, like it or not, it's out of . . . it's out of your hands. Triffin and his mother are coming over tomorrow afternoon to talk about it, and you'll be polite whether you like it or not. And this discussion is over."

I thought about pulling a Katie Hardcastle and having the last word, but then I remembered that my dad isn't Mr. Sigsworth. I mean, for one thing Mr. Sigsworth doesn't control my pocket money.

14 THE BIGGER, STUPIDER IDEA

That Sunday Nerdstrom and his mother came to visit, which was about as much fun as having your teeth pulled out with rusty pliers. I heard their old orange Volvo approaching from heaps far away, and I was cross even before I heard the car doors go creak and bang out in the driveway.

Mum went and answered the door, of course, and I was upstairs with Cameron, watching from my bedroom window as Mrs. Nordstrom tried to convince her pathetic son to get out of the car.

"What are they coming for, exactly?" Cameron asked.

"Don't worry about it," I said.

But he wouldn't give up. "Why is Nerdstrom coming to *our* house?"

"Shut up," I said.

"Don't tell me you're *friends* with Nerdstrom. He's such a *lamo!*" Cameron said, and I frowned at him.

"Do you remember him?"

Cameron rolled his eyes at me and said, "Duh! Me and Andy Little flushed his head like *heaps* of times when I was in sixth grade. And now you're friends with him! That's hilarious!"

I shook my head. "I'm not friends with him," I said, but Cameron wasn't convinced.

"So why is he even here?" he asked.

"Shut up."

We went out into the upstairs hallway and listened. We heard Mum open the door, and then she was all, "Oh, well, hello! How nice to see you again! Come in!"

"Good morning, how are you?" I heard Mrs. Nordstrom say. "Oh, what a lovely home!" Which is probably true, when you compare it to the hippie shack that she and Nerdstrom live in, but it's hardly worth an exclamation mark.

But Mum didn't mind hearing about how nice our house is. She went, "Oh, thank you, thank you so much. We do what we can. Hello, Triffin, how *are* you?"

That was when Cameron said, in this really low voice, "Yep, your boyfriend's here, Maxine," and I shoved him hard in the chest, making him sit down awkwardly in the middle of the hallway.

Mum started calling me. "Max. Max? Max, your guest is here." Guest? *I* never invited him. But I went down the stairs, and when I got to the bottom I saw the two of them and Mum standing in the entryway. Mrs. Nordstrom was carrying a basket with a couple of covered bowls in it, and I quickly glanced in to make sure that she had no evil-smelling green juice in there. Luckily the only thing that I could see that looked green was Nerdstrom's face.

"Good morning, Max," Nerdstrom's mum said, and I did a pretty good job of smiling and being polite, I thought. "It's very nice to see you again," she said.

It's only nice to see you again if you definitely don't have any wheatgrass and celery juice in that basket, I thought. But of course I never said it. I just smiled politely some more.

Then Nerdstrom looked at me from under his eyebrows and said, "Max."

"Nerd . . . Triffin," I said. Then there was a long pause, and neither of us knew what to say. But finally Mum flashed a quick little smile and said, "Well, why don't we sit down in the living room?"

Because we'd all rather fish our own brains out through our nostrils with chopsticks, I thought. But, like before, I knew better than to say it.

Bamboo brain-removers. (tried out on Jared first.) ((very little to remove.))

Then Mum said, "Max, do you mind letting your father know that our guests are here? He's out back cleaning the gutters." As I headed for the back door, I heard her say, "He knew you were coming, Ulrika, but sometimes he gets a bee in his bonnet."

Dad was up a ladder, and when I told him that our visitors had arrived, he took a deep breath and said, "I'd rather finish this." That surprised me, because Dad hates working around the house, especially when it involves ladders. Ever since that incident with the so-called nonslip shoes, he'd never quite trusted them.

But he came down, very carefully, and washed his hands at the outside tap before we went inside. "Try to understand, mate," he said, as we came through the back door, and I wasn't quite sure what he meant by that. There were two Nordstroms on our couch—how could I ever understand something like that? But there was no time to ask, because a couple of seconds later we were in the living room, and Dad was shaking hands with Mrs. Nordstrom while Nerdstrom himself sat on the couch and looked at his hands and Mum made tea in the kitchen.

Eventually we were all sitting together. The grown-ups had tea, Nerdstrom and I had juice, and there were some crackers and a bowl of strong-smelling green paste in the middle of the table. I guessed that Mrs. Nordstrom had brought that along. I didn't know where my brother was, and I didn't want to know, as long as he wasn't there to witness my embarrassment.

Then Mrs. Nordstrom said, "So, should we get started?"

"At what?" I asked.

Both my parents frowned at me then, which didn't seem fair. I wasn't being rude, and I think it's a reasonable question when someone says, "Let's get started." At what? Twister? Croquet? Clearing the room with a freshly opened canister of tear gas?

Mrs. Nordstrom cleared her throat, then she said, "Now, boys, as your parents we're concerned about a couple of things—"

"Like what?" I interrupted.

But she held up one hand and tilted her chin away from me, and said, "We're concerned about a couple of things, and I just want you both to know that your teacher and your principal know about what we're discussing today."

Great, I thought. Mr. Sigsworth, Mrs. Bryce, and three parents add up to at least five people so far who know more than me and possibly Nerdstrom.

Nerdstrom's mum was still talking. "Now Max, you're good at schoolwork, we know you are, because you've got a good brain, but it seems that you're not trying very hard, especially in math, from what your parents tell me. Is that true?"

I just shrugged, even though she was right so far. I do have a good brain, and I don't try very hard in math. But I didn't want her to think that she'd worked me out straight away. Besides, what was of more interest to me at that moment was why she was doing all the talking, while Mum sat on the edge of her seat with her tea balanced on her knee and Dad sat back in his chair with a mouthful of Anzac biscuit.

She just carried on, ignoring my shrug. "Okay, good. And Triffin, you're good at math, aren't you?"

As if you don't know that, I thought. Of course he's good at math—just look at him. Then Nerdstrom nodded, but I think he was embarrassed to actually admit it, which is why he made a noise that sounded a bit like he was clearing his throat, but not much more than that. So Mrs. Nordstrom said again,

"Okay, good. But Triffin, it seems to me that you've been having some trouble fitting in at school. Do you think that's true?" And he made the throat noise again. "Okay, excellent. Max, what do you think *you're* good at?" I shrugged again.

Why was *she* doing all the talking? My parents weren't saying a thing, and we were in our fairly normal house, not her weird little rattly one, so shouldn't they have been allowed to speak?

But she wasn't going to be put off by me responding with shrugs. She said, "No, you *do* know, Max. What are you good at? Tell me. I'd like to know." She was sitting forward in her chair, so she was actually kind of looking up into my face. Plus her head was bent to one side, which I really hate.

What was I good at? "Sports and stuff, I guess," I said. "And there's this thing I can do with my armpit—"

She interrupted me then, and asked, "Is there anything else?" But I shrugged again, so she gave me a hint. She said, "Do you think you're good at people stuff?"

I thought about this. People stuff? That was an odd way to put it, I thought, but maybe I was.

"Being a leader, maybe?" she said. "Hmm? Do you

think that's a fair comment? That maybe you're good at persuading people?"

And she really had me there. She *did* know me after all. I *was* good at those things, so I nodded and said, "Yeah, I am good at stuff like that. Especially the convincing bit." But Nerdstrom didn't seem all that convinced, because he was just staring at the floor like he was looking for a safe place to spew.

Then Mrs. Nordstrom said, "So it looks like we all have something to offer, don't we?" I'm pretty sure that was a rhetorical question, and I think Nerdstrom thought it was too, because me and him both didn't say anything. But his mum still went on talking anyway. "Because you each have something to offer the other, here's what Max's parents and I think we should do. Max, Triffin is going to give you some extra help with your math. Twice a week you're going to go to the library together, and he's going to help you."

"The kids are going to make so much fun of me," I said.

Then Mum spoke up. "We've already arranged it with your teacher, Max, and he's going to keep this to himself. He's promised to be very discreet, and I do trust Darrell Sigsworth. We all do. So what do you think? Agreed?"

I wanted to ask if I had a choice, but as soon as I snuck a glance at my parents and saw Dad's face I knew that it wouldn't do any good, so instead I just nodded. If I hadn't nodded I think that maybe I would've cried, and there was no way I was going to give Nerdstrom *that* kind of satisfaction. And crying sucks anyway.

"Excellent," Mrs. Nordstrom said. "And here's the other part of the deal. Every weekend you two boys are going to spend some time together. One weekend here at Max's place, the next weekend at our place."

What? Were they serious? I looked at Nerdstrom to see if he was as surprised and peed off as I was about this amazing plan, but his face was blank.

So then I looked at my parents. Mum had a kind of half smile on her face, but it was one I hadn't seen before. And Dad was looking kind of worried, as if he wasn't sure if this plan was such a great idea after all. But he didn't speak up, which made me even more mad. If he thought it was as dopey a plan as I did, why didn't he open his mouth and say something?

"I won't do it," I said. "I won't do it at all. I'm not having . . . *him* teaching me math."

Mrs. Nordstrom smiled at me. "It won't be that bad—you'll see."

So I tried Mum next. I said, "Mum, are you guys serious about this?"

She just nodded. "It's going to be fine, you'll see." The last time she said that was just before she took my guinea pig, Murray, to the vet and he never came home, so it shouldn't have been a surprise that I didn't trust her.

"Dad?" I said, but he just shook his head slowly.

"Sorry, mate. It's a done deal."

Then I did something I never thought I'd do. I actually tried to get Nerdstrom and me on the same side. I said to him, "What do *you* think of this? Don't you think this is a stupid idea?"

And he looked up and stared me right in the eye. "Yup," he said.

15 NERDSTROM TALKS ABOUT ATTITUDE

That Monday I ran into Nerdstrom at the front of our classroom, where all the bags were hanging. I was taking Heather Manning's lame pink bag off the hook closest to the door and hanging my own on it, when he walked up, and as usual I saw him hesitate just a tiny bit. "Max," he said.

"Nerdstrom."

When we both remembered the conversation at my place the day before, there was this embarrassed silence between us, like that time I broke up with Imogen Broadleigh after we'd been going out for two days, three hours, and twenty-eight minutes. Eventually I thought one of us should be the grownup and say something, so I did. I said, "This is so dumb. Like I want to learn math from *you!*"

"Yeah, and hanging out with *you* every weekend is going to be a barrel of monkeys as well," he muttered, which is a pretty weird and Nerdstrom-y kind of thing to say, if you ask me.

"So how are we going to get around this?" I asked him.

Barrel of munk monkeys. (what the?)

He shrugged and said, "I don't think I can. I don't think *we* can. We have to just do it."

"But why *you?*" I asked.

He just shook his head and said, "Because I'm good at math. And because our parents think it would be good for both of us to spend some time together, I guess. My mum's a couselor thing, and she thinks that I need to confront my fears head-on or something."

"Aha!" I said. "You *are* scared of me!"

He didn't even blink. "They were her words, not mine. So why do you think they wanted to stick us together? You don't like me, and I don't like you very much either."

How should I know why they wanted us hanging out together? What a dopey question! It really did seem to me like the stupidest idea in the history of the modern age. Sort of like putting a pitbull in a cage with a poodle and expecting them both to be alive the next day. Or like asking Gladys Mulholland from our grade to decorate a cake and hoping to have any cake left at the end.

Excited Gladys.

Nervous cake.

"The only way it's going to work is if no one finds out about it," I said. "*No* one."

Then Nerdstrom said something that I thought was quite mean. "Suits me," he said. "Why would I want people to know that I was hanging out with *you?*"

"I don't know," I said.

But it turned out that he was actually being all shrewd and clever and rhetorical, because he answered his own question. "I wouldn't. Hanging out with you? No way. I've got a reputation to maintain."

During recess I asked Mr. Sigsworth if I could talk to him, and he said I could. But first I had to tell Jared to leave us alone, because I definitely didn't want him to know about the math thing.

But Jared just looked puzzled. "Why do I have to go?"

"Because I told you to," I said.

"Just for a minute, Jared," said Mr. Sigsworth.

Once Jared had finished rolling his eyes and left, I asked Mr. Sigsworth about the big plan with me and Nerdstrom.

"Because you each have something to offer the other," he said. "You need help with your math— yes, you do, Max—and Triffin needs confidence.

And I'd consider it a personal favor if you didn't rock the boat too much about this."

"But what about spending the weekends together?" I asked.

"That's something your parents thought of," he said. Then he put a hand on my shoulder and said, "It'll be fine, Max."

That's what *you* reckon, I thought, and you'll see what a disaster this'll end up being.

But I didn't say it, because even though he was part of this stupid plan, I actually think he's an okay teacher, apart from wearing too much aftershave and having Darrell for a first name.

16 THE RECRUIT

That Tuesday I saw the first grade kid from detention again. He was out on the playground with one of his little friends, and even though I think all first grade kids look pretty much the same, I recognized him straight away. Maybe it was because Mr. Goward was telling him off about something and he wasn't even crying. Usually if a teacher wants to make a kid cry, all they have to do is say "Excuse me, young man, did I just see what I thought I saw?" or "You two boys over there, I want to see you right now." It's often enough to just look at them in a particular way. But not this kid. Mr. Goward was really up in his face, and I don't know what it was that he'd done, but from what Jared and I could hear as we walked past, it involved girls, skirts, and spiders, which made me respect that kid right away. Even though there was a teacher in there giving him a complete shouting-at, he was hardly even blinking or anything. He was just like, "Uh-huh, okay, no worries."

I liked that kid immediately.

After Mr. Goward had finished with the kid and he had gone off picking up lunch papers as his punishment, I started to walk toward him.

"What are you doing?" Jared asked, as if it was impossible to believe that I would actually *want* to talk to a first grade kid, but I just ignored him. Sometimes that's the best way to deal with Jared.

I went up to the kid and said, "What's going on?"

Which probably seems like a dumb question, but asking that usually gives me a chance to see how a kid is going to cope with being talked to by someone who's going to be in seventh grade next year. The thing is, if they cry, then I know they're just normal, and they're harmless. If they go, "I'm picking up papers, stupid. What does it look like?" then I know they're little upstarts who need to become the focus of a campaign of terror. But if they show a blend of respect and confidence when directly addressed by someone like me, then I know that they're the kind of person I can get to know. Especially if I've got some kind of objective I want to accomplish in the school. See, it's always good to have someone on the inside when it comes to operating in circles you don't usually hang out in, like first grade.

So anyway, I said to this kid, "What's going on?" and he just shrugged and muttered something that I couldn't quite hear. And that seemed to me to be disrespectful, and so was the mutter, so I should have just gone straight to the campaign of terror, but there was something about the *way* he shrugged, something that said, "I know I'm picking up papers, but I'm not quite sure why." Which I thought was kind of cool, so I decided to give him another chance.

"Why are you picking up papers?"

He shrugged again and said, "I'm being punished by *him.*"

When he said *him* and just pointed with his chin at Mr. Goward, I knew he was probably okay, so I asked, "What's your name, kid?"

"Casey Reeves," he said. "I know you—you're Max Quigley. I was in detention with you the other day."

"Yes, I remember you, Reeves. You were in detention two days in a row. What did you do—wet your pants?"

But he just sniffed, and gave a chuckly little laugh and said, "No, I was starting fires in the toilets. You didn't hear about that?"

I was shocked. This was big news that I hadn't heard. "No, no one told me about fires in toilets. Was anyone hurt?" I asked, and when Casey shook his head, I went, "Still, sounds cool."

I looked at Jared, who was standing nearby with a very slight smile on his dopey face. I knew what he was thinking, too. He was thinking that we'd just got ourselves a recruit.

17 MR. SIGSWORTH SCREWS UP

Except for the aftershave, Mr. Sigsworth is an okay guy, and he might even be a pretty good teacher, despite the plan he'd helped cook up with my parents and Nerdstrom's mum. He's not quite as much fun as Mr. Steinmuller in fourth grade, who can do strange voices and play the guitar heaps good, and if Mr. Sigsworth did those things it would just look like he was copying, and then he wouldn't look cool anyway.

Even though Mr. Sigsworth's mostly okay, sometimes I think his brain might stop working, just for a little while. I mean, what other explanation can there be for what happened at two o'clock that Wednesday afternoon? Me and Nerdstrom both knew that at two o'clock we should just pack our things up without any fuss and go over to the library, which is where the whole "tutoring" thing was supposed to happen. Mr. Sigsworth knew about that plan as well, after he got a long note signed by Nerdstrom's mum and my parents, asking him to be discreet or something. He'd even told us. He'd said, "It's okay, I've spoken to all of your parents, and I'm going to be very discreet."

I was already worried about the other kids asking why we were going to the library anyway, but I'd taken Nerdstrom somewhere quiet at recess and said that if anyone asked, he had to tell them that he was having an extra violin lesson, and I'd tell them that I was going to the principal's office to report in, sort of like a parole thing. So Nerdstrom agreed (even though I don't think he liked the idea much) and that was all kind of sorted out.

That is, I *thought* it was sorted out until Mr. Sigsworth said, at about five minutes to two, "Triffin, Max, don't forget your appointment at two." Then he handed us a bright yellow library pass, and I was surprised, then confused, then shocked, and finally peed right off, especially when a couple of the other kids started going, "Ooooo! Triffin and Quigley in the li-bra-ry, K-I-S-S-I-N-G."

Then Josh Hargreaves said, "How come *they* get to go to the library while we have to stay here and do math?" I was holding my breath waiting for Mr. Sigsworth's answer. And guess what it was? I couldn't believe my ears! He actually said, "Don't worry, they'll be doing math as well, Josh." I mean, hello! *Everyone* knows that Nerdstrom is really good at math and I'm like, well, unmotivated. So it was really obvious to *everyone* in the class that scaredy little Treefern Nerdstrom was going to be helping big, stupid Max Dumbo Quigley with his math.

I held Mr. Sigsworth responsible. Why even have a plan at all if you're going to just stomp all over it on the first day? Even if you are an okay teacher, which I thought he was.

Anyway, me and Nerdstrom went into the library, and I was feeling all kinds of embarrassed, but when we walked in we were the only ones there except for a bunch of littlies over in the picture book section. And there were these two kids who were kind of wrestling with each other, and the librarian went over and totally ripped into them, which was heaps funny.

I wanted to stay and watch, but Nerdstrom was all, "Come on, I'd like to get this over with," like it was going to be more of a big deal for him than for me.

So we gave our library pass to Mrs. Lalor, who's the grouchy old library assistant who always makes the photocopier stop working, and found a table in

Mrs Lalor about to fix the photocopier.

Paper here

the corner. Nerdstrom sat down, and I sat down, and he opened up a folder and took out all these pages and stuck them in front of me and said, in this trembly kind of voice, "This is what Sigsy gave me to do with you."

"I don't want you to help me," I said.

"I know, and the feeling's mutual." Then he coughed a bit, and said, "I don't think you need my help anyway."

"You're right," I said. "I don't."

And I thought he might leave it there, but he didn't. He said, "Because I think you're just lazy, and since I was forced into this just as much as you were, why don't you start doing the questions while I sit here and read my book, and if you have any questions you can talk to me then. But I don't want to talk about anything else." And he took out some fat, nerdy fantasy book the size of a brick and started reading, probably hoping I wouldn't notice how much he was blushing.

But I said, "Whoa, whoa. Back up, Nerdstrom. Did you just call him *Sigsy?*"

"Yeah, so what? Everyone calls him that. *You* call him that."

"Yeah, I know, but I'm me, and you're you. So don't try to be cool when you're not."

But then he said maybe the most annoying thing of all. He went, "Listen, don't get mad or anything, but I reckon the sooner you start improving at your *math,* the sooner we can go back to living our separate lives. And I think we both want our weekends back, don't we?"

And I nodded, which especially annoyed me, having to agree with him, but it was a fair point.

"Fine, read your stupid fat geek book," I said, which maybe wasn't the cleverest thing I could have said, but I was caught out by this sudden attitude that Nerdstrom was giving me, and I had to think of something fast. I did make a mental note to sort him out properly once I'd done my time at Camp Nerdstrom, however.

So there I was, sitting there trying to figure out these math questions. Or half trying, anyway, because the other half of me was trying to work out how I could get right under Nerdstrom's skin without making him refuse to help me. And I was having a hard time. I mean, I was having a hard time with *both* those things. The math was hard enough, but then there was the other thing, and both together meant that my brain was starting to kind of wrinkle at the edges. So I looked up at Nerdstrom, and he was deep in his book, which had this really stupid picture of some guy in armor sitting on a horse, and they were standing in front of this huge mountain with snow on the top. Actually, it looked pretty cool, but I figured that since it was Nerdstrom's it probably couldn't be.

Then he noticed me watching him and looked up, and I said, "You know, I could use some help here, Nerdstrom."

He sighed, slid a bookmark into his book, and put it down on the desk. "All right, but remember that *you* asked *me* for help. So if you tell anyone that I *wanted* to help you, I'll deny it." Which is just ridiculous, because I certainly didn't intend to discuss it with anyone to begin with, and he should have known that.

So he leaned over and got his pencil and just kind of went, "This one here? Okay, the five will only go into eight once, so that means there's how many left over?"

And I said, "After you take out five?" and he nodded, and I said, "Three."

"Right. So the three goes there, which makes the five into thirty-five, doesn't it?"

And that was when I saw what he was doing, and said, "So that means if five goes into thirty-five seven times, the answer is seventeen, isn't it?"

And Nerdstrom could have been a total jerk and

gone "Duh!" or "Oh, aren't you a clever boy!" or something like that, but he didn't. He just nodded and said, "There you go," before going back to his book with the knight on the front.

Then I said, "Have you thought about what you're going to do for our assembly? Has Sigsy talked to you about that? Because you were away the day he told us."

"How do you know I was away?" Nerdstrom asked. "Have you been stalking me?"

"As if," I said. "So has he told you about it or not?"

I was enjoying watching Nerdstrom's shape change. He was starting to look like some of the air had leaked out of him. "Yeah, he's told me."

"So what are you going to do?" I asked. I pointed at his book. "You going to bore everyone to death with tales of swords and spells and Klingons?"

A wand, NOT a sparkler

One of Nerdstrom's fantasy Klingons. (LAME!)

Max

That got his attention, and some of his air seemed to come back. "Klingons are actually from *Star Trek*, not fantasy, and I don't even *like Star Trek* all that much. And no, I don't think I'm going to bore anyone to death. I'm working on it. Don't worry about it, okay?"

"Does it scare you, performing in front of all those people?" I asked, because I knew that it did.

Nerdstrom looked me right in the eye and said, "You *know* it does. I'm reading now. Leave me alone."

So I did. But I knew I'd made him think.

Later, when the bell rang, I said to Nerdstrom, "You go out first."

"Why?"

"Because neither of us wants to draw attention to this whole math thing, do we? So we should leave separately, to avoid people noticing." After some of the attitude he'd been giving me, I totally expected him to tell me not to be stupid, but he didn't.

Later, when I was picking up my bag and stuff from the classroom, Jared came up to me and said, "So, how was your vege-math class?"

And I said, "I don't know what you're talking about."

But he didn't believe me at all, and he said, "I know what's going on. I worked it out, after what Sigsy said."

"It's not what you think," I said, but Jared just smiled.

"I think Nerdstrom's helping you with your math. Why else would you go to the library together?"

"If you tell anyone . . ."

"You'll what?" He laughed. "The thing is, you and Nerdstrom doing math together just doesn't . . . well, it doesn't *add up!*" Then he totally cracked up.

Although Jared is definitely my best friend in the whole world and always will be, I was so close to punching him in the head right then. But I didn't, because there were heaps of people around, and that's the only reason.

And anyway, like I keep explaining, that's not my style.

18 CAMERON LEARNS (SOME OF) THE TRUTH

That Thursday I had a meat pie for lunch, and it was nice. It actually was.

What wasn't nice is how the night before went. Mum and Dad asked me how the first day of tutoring had gone. That would have been okay, except they asked at dinner time, and of course Cameron was there, and he didn't know about the tutoring yet, and his ears pricked up. "What's this about tutoring?"

"Just forget it," I said, but of course Cameron wasn't going to just forget it, because he's like a guard dog who can smell fear, except I wasn't scared. But he knew it was a sensitive subject, so he just waded in.

"Oh, is little Maxine finding school difficult? You do know what *difficult* means, don't you, Maxine? It's a big word, a grown-up word that means *hard*. That's right, *hard,* as in *not easy.*"

Mum was shaking her head at him and telling him

to stop, but Cameron doesn't listen to Mum very much, so he just kept going.

That's when Dad said, "Cameron, that's enough. We just thought that Triffin and Max could offer each other something valuable."

As soon as Cameron heard Dad say "Triffin," it was like he'd just been given free tickets to Disneyland. "Triffin? *Triffin!* You're being taught math by *Nerdstrom?* That's why he was here the other day?"

"How do you know Triffin?" Mum asked him.

"How do I know Triffin?" said Cameron (which is a really dumb thing to say, since he was just repeating exactly what she'd said. And it's not really even rhetorical, because he was just repeating exactly what she'd said). "I know Nerdstrom because I used to see him all the time before I went to high school. I remember this one time . . ." And then he started laughing so hard that I thought mashed potato was going to come out his nose. Once he'd managed to stop laughing, he told us all some story about the time he helped these other boys flush Nerdstrom's head. I mean, *I* thought it was pretty funny, but Mum and Dad just looked annoyed.

When Cameron had finished his story, Dad cleared his throat and said, "Are you done, Cameron? Can we finish our dinner without stories about heads in toilets? Thank you." It was hard for me and Cameron not to look at each other and laugh like mad. But at least Cameron seemed to have forgotten about me being taught math by someone my own age.

Or so I thought. After dinner I was in my room and Cameron came in, or rather he just stood at the door, and he said, "So, how is my old buddy Nerdstrom? Is he really as smart as they say? I mean, he's only teaching *you,* so how smart would he have to be?" Which was so funny that I thought I might actually stop breathing, I was laughing so hard. Not.

So I said, "Hey, it's okay. You know why? Because I'm letting him think that I'm fine with him helping me, but that just lets me get close to him so that when the time comes to really sort him out, he won't suspect a thing."

Cameron just laughed. "Kind of like one of those keep your friends close, your enemies even closer things?"

"Yeah, exactly like that."

Cameron just shook his head and went off to his own room. Sometimes I really hate him.

But he hadn't mentioned the weekend visits, so I guessed that he didn't know about *those* yet. And I wasn't in any big rush to tell him, either. I figured he'd find out soon enough.

So, it looked like I'd be doing tutoring with Nerdstrom twice a week, on Wednesdays and Fridays, and I wasn't even sure how long for. I asked Mr. Sigsworth that, and he said that he'd be keeping his eye on my progress and staying in contact with our parents, which I thought might have been his way of saying "I haven't really thought about it yet."

Typical.

19 THE DEVELOPMENT OF CASEY

That Friday I had tutoring again, and it was okay, I guess. Nerdstrom was still the same. He just sat down opposite me in the library and said, "I'm reading. Don't disturb me unless it's something really hard."

"Hard for me or hard for you?"

"Just don't disturb me unless you think your head's going to explode."

And that was when I wished I *could* make my head explode, just to see the look on his face. But then I'd have an exploded head, and it would be hard to see anything, which would be inconvenient, but it would be almost worth it just to imagine the freaked-out look on his face.

There was something else. A couple of the other kids had already caught on to what was going on, and were calling Nerdstom "The Professor." I didn't start it, though. Well, not on purpose, anyway. I might have accidentally called him Prof when we were lining up for assembly. And sometimes that's all it takes.

Casey Reeves is pretty cool, it turns out. He'd come over to see us from time to time, but not too much. I mean, I certainly didn't want some first grade kid hanging around all the time, but with him it was like having a really cool pet, like a snake or a performing tarantula who eats mice whenever your friends come over. I could just kind of say, "Hey Casey, I dare you to go over there and tip that girl's drink over," and he'd totally do it, and he didn't even say I'd told him to, which was great.

The thing was, I had Casey completely convinced that if he wanted to keep being the toughest little kid in the school, he had to do whatever the toughest kid in the *whole* school told him to do, so long as it was a dare. And that toughest kid was me, and Jared sort of, especially when I was away. And that kind of dare was totally safe for me, because even if Casey did tell the teachers that I'd dared him, I probably wasn't going to get a detention for it, and Casey was just going to get told not to listen to older kids like me. So it was all good. And Casey did whatever I dared him to do, and a couple of times he even got put in detention because of stuff I told him to do.

But he never even blamed me, which was the best thing of all, like I said.

20 APRIL FOOLS' DAY

That Saturday Dad was away on his Army Reserve weekend. He left on Friday afternoon, all dressed up in his soldier stuff looking like a hero, to be honest. (Not a very smart hero, obviously, since he had a badge reading QUIGLEY stitched on his shirt, just in case he forgot his name.) The last thing he said to me as he went to get into his mate Ernie's car was that I should be good. "Your mum's got her Natureway Cosmetics party tomorrow, so behave, all right?" he said.

Yeah yeah yeah, blah blah blah, I was thinking. What he'd forgotten was that Saturday was April Fools' Day. Having April the first on a Saturday was probably a good thing for a number of kids at school. It's safer for them that way, with kids like me and Jared on the loose. Plus they don't have to strain their brains trying to work out which of the announce-ments are real and which ones are the teachers playing jokes. Like the principal, Mrs. Bryce, announcing that the pet elephants are *not* to be sponged down in the girls' toilets under *any circumstances,* for example. Hilarious.

Normally I love April Fools' Day. Take last year, for example. It's amazing the different responses you see when someone sets off the fire alarms at school just as everyone is coming out for lunch. For a start there's the screaming, panicky stampede, which is kind of cool, except for that one person who sort of got crushed in the mad rush. But seriously, who comes to school with crutches? If you've suffered an injury that makes crutches necessary, you should be making the most of that and not coming to school at all. But when you're the only person out of all the staff who knows how to make the computers work in the library, I suppose it's best that you make the effort to come to school. Even with crutches. And especially if you've been using crutches to get around since you were four. But you shouldn't be trying to carry an iMac as well as use crutches. I mean, that's just stupid.

There are a few different responses you get from the teachers when someone presses the fire alarm. Some of them scream and run with the kids. Others stand in the middle of the hall and shout, "Don't panic! Remain calm!" Some look wide-eyed and pale, as if this is the single worst nightmare they've ever had in school. And there are some teachers who actually do remain calm and say to the kids, "All right, just leave your bags and go out into the quad. It might be a real fire or it might be a false alarm, but we'll work that out later. It's okay, Amanda, there *are* no real elephants." They're the boring ones.

Then there's Mrs. Bryce. She's the one who stands in the quad directing the teachers and telling *them* to remain calm. She's also the one who talks to the firemen in their stupid yellow pants and jackets for a while, then starts turning slowly in a circle, going, "Where's Max Quigley?"

The worst thing is that all this happened just before midday and ended about half an hour after midday, so by the time I got to actually say "April fool!" it was too late. That's one of the April Fools' Day rules. Which is probably why Mrs. Bryce didn't laugh when I said it. Neither did the boss of the firemen.

But the most disturbing reaction was from my parents, who didn't see the funny side of it either. I'm not sure how many hundred dollars it costs for two fire engines to come out to our school for a false

alarm, but I do know that I didn't get any pocket money for most of last year.

Since April 1 this year was on a Saturday, like I said, I wasn't at school. Also, I was still grounded from baseball, so I couldn't even do anything there. So I had to settle for getting out of bed early and sneaking into Cameron's bedroom with a bowl of warm water, and gently lowering his hand into it. He didn't even wake up when he wet his pajama pants, and I was able to sneak back out and dispose of the evidence. Then, at breakfast, I asked him why he had a morning shower instead of an evening one. He said it was none of my business, and I said, "Which little piggy are you?"

"Huh?"

I said, "Was it the one that went *wee wee wee wee* all the way home?"

Then he looked really cross, and I said, "Don't get peed off," and he looked even crankier.

"Do you know anything about this?" he asked.

And I said, "No, but I do know that it's April Fools' Day. Ha!"

Then Mum said, "Max, I hope you haven't forgotten that Triffin's coming over later."

Cameron totally cracked up. "That's great, Mum!

Look at his face! Triffin's coming over! Ha-ha, ha-ha! April fool, Maxine!"

But it wasn't an April Fools' Day joke, even though I wished it were, and once Cameron realized that Nerdstrom really *was* coming over for some of the day, he started laughing even more, which made my knuckles start to clench and my nostrils start to flare in and out.

Maybe it was this start to the day that led Mum to tell me and Cameron that once her party kicked off, we weren't to come out into the living room under any circumstances. Mum told us this as she was getting ready to drive down to the shops to pick up a couple of bottles of wine. "Listen, I don't want you two screwing it up for me, all right?" she said. "Triffin's going to be here with you, and I want you to show him a good example, especially since Ulrika's going to stay for the party. I don't want any monkey business."

"Who's Ulrika?" Cameron asked.

"Nerdstrom's mum," I said, and Cameron looked like he was going to start laughing all over again.

Then Mum said, "I'm serious, boys. Because your father's not here to watch you, I need you to promise not to do anything terrible."

Of course we both promised, which is something that doesn't mean anything except, "Yes Mum, we can see how important it is to you that you think we promise."

After that Mum sort of relaxed her face and said, "This is really big for me. I've got a couple of new people coming today, and I really want to get to the next level before the big Natureway conference in Brisbane." This was a very unusual thing to say. She made her business sound like a computer game. The next level? Is that the one where you have to depong the monsters with antipong aftershave and treat all their zits with antizit loofa scrubs? Probably.

Yes, the situation was very clear to me, and just as

clear to Cameron once I'd explained it to him. Obviously our mother was embarrassed by her own kids! She would rather that we sat in our rooms being bored out of our minds rather than risk that we would make her feel ashamed of us. Which is twice as bad when you think that we've got a perfectly good 106-cm widescreen LCD TV down there in the living room, and a surround-sound system, plus about a hundred DVDs that are achieving nothing while they remain unwatched in their boxes. Making us stay away from that part of the house on a Sunday is like leaving a bottle of water just out of the reach of a man who's dying of thirst. Or putting a locked glass case full of chocolates in Gladys Mulholland's bedroom.

So to sum up, not only was our mother ashamed of her own children, but she thought it was okay to torture them as well, just so she could get what *she* wanted.

Anyway, me and Cameron weren't very happy that we'd been banned from the one room in the house that contained the most interesting stuff, especially on a day when she might have been busy enough to forget that I wasn't allowed to watch TV. Besides, there was a principle at stake. So we decided between us that a plan was required, especially since it was the

first day of April, and since we had to set a good example for our guest.

Cameron's not usually all that great at coming up with plans. He's more of a follower. But this time, he was the one with the big light bulb going off above his head. He said, "Hey, Max, what's the smelliest thing you can think of, apart from you?"

I suggested all the usual smelly things, but he just smiled and shook his head, and kept smiling and shaking his head every time I suggested something, until I threatened to hold him down and dribble on him.

"No, it has to be liquid, like perfume," he said. "You know, all yellow."

I somehow resisted the urge to remind him about the hand-in-warm-water incident and instead said, "How about *real* perfume?"

"No, stupid, just think about it. Just imagine if someone got out a bottle of this really expensive perfume, and put some here and here"—he sort of pretended to dab some behind his ears, then on his wrists—"and once they put it on they realized that it was actually something really stinky, like salad dressing . . ."

"It's not just perfume that Mum's selling," I said. There were all these creams and things as well, all in

their little tubes and tubs and stuff. And these were the tubes and tubs and stuff that Mum was going to use to demonstrate her products to the other ladies. And that was the plan, right there, staring us in the face.

We knew that we had to move quickly. I mean, the wine shop that Mum was going to was a fair ways away, and she had a few other things she had to pick up from the supermarket as well, but we didn't want her walking in to find us scraping out her tub of defoliating facial scrub and filling it with hummus (which is the stinky garlicky paste that Mum likes on her crackers instead of Nutella). And speaking of Nutella, we thought about using that to replace the jojoba rejuvenating facemask pack, but the color was all wrong, plus it would have been a waste of good Nutella, so in the end we just went with extra-smooth peanut butter. And once you've squeezed out a tube of moisturizing exfoliant skin toner, it's amazing how hard it is to get satay sauce back in through the little hole. But we managed.

And the perfume? Well *that* was easy, after everything else. We used a dribble from the half-finished bottle of home-brewed beer that Dad had left in the fridge. It was the right color and everything.

We really wanted to be nearby to watch the car-

nage that was sure to unfold, but we're not complete idiots. We knew that Mum would get more suspicious if we were hanging around, especially because Cameron giggles when someone's about to discover one of his pranks, so in the end we decided that we would just have to enjoy the experience from the safety of our rooms.

So me and Cameron went into my room, and we secretly played some games on my PlayStation, and a little later, when I was about halfway through that level of *Martial Law IV* where the drug dealers drive into the alleyway in their black Mercedes and start shooting wildly, I heard a car door slam.

"They're here," I said.

And Cameron said, "So start shooting back!"

"No, I mean the perfume ladies are here."

I paused the game and we went over to the window. A red car was out front, and two ladies got out. One of them was heaps skinny, and kind of sharp-looking around the edges, and Cameron said, "She looks like she needs some peanut butter on that face of hers," which totally cracked me up.

As they were walking up the driveway, just looking around at the garden the way people do, another car pulled up. It was a silver four-wheel-drive, and two more ladies got out. The first two, who were almost at our front door by then, turned around, and they must have known the new arrivals, because they were all kissy-kissy and going, "How *are* you, darling?" (which was probably rhetorical, since they didn't even wait to hear the answer).

All of this made Cameron go, "How are *you, darling?*" and try to kiss me, which was creepy and random and actually quite scary. So I pushed him away and he kind of fell over the end of his bed, and that was when he punched me really hard in the chest, which hurt.

Then the doorbell rang downstairs, and we snuck out into the upstairs hallway and to the top of the stairs so we could hear better, and of course once Mum went and opened the door all the kissy-kissy stuff started all over again, and me and Cameron were thinking that this was the dumbest, most embarrassing display we'd ever seen.

Then we heard another voice at the door, which was Mrs. Nordstrom's, and she was saying, in her crazy accent, "Hello, Julianne, how lovely to see you. Thank you so much for inviting me to stay."

For a minute I thought that maybe Ulrika had forgotten to bring Nerdstrom along, which would have been fantastic, but then I heard Mum say, "The boys are just upstairs, Triffin. Up you go. Max's room is the second one on the right."

"Great," I said under my breath, and I heard Cameron stiffling a giggle. "It totally wasn't my idea," I said.

And next thing we knew, Nerdstrom was coming up the stairs. He looked like an apprentice lion tamer about to tame his first lion, and I guess we looked like the lions.

I said, "So you came then."

Nerdstrom grunted something.

Then Cameron said, "I've got some math I need help with," and I thumped him while Nerdstrom just kind of blinked.

"Hi, Cameron," Nerdstrom said.

"So do you remember each other?" I asked.

"How could I forget?" Nerdstrom replied.

Cameron said, "You look kind of flushed."

A quick, tense smile flickered across Nerdstrom's face. "Yes, I remember you used to say that when you were at our school. It really does get more hilarious every time I hear it."

And even though I thought that was pretty funny, I didn't want to show it, and when Cameron made a seriously threatening face I started to think that Nerdstrom's visit might not last all that long after all, because he was probably going to run crying downstairs and beg his mummy to take him home.

But there was fun to be had, so I said, "Okay, cool it down, you guys. Nerdstrom, the excitement is about to begin."

"What excitement?" he asked, all nervous, like I meant that the fun involved clothespins and him.

"No, nothing like that," I said, and I told him how we'd swapped the face creams and things. And I think he did actually find it funny. Not *really* funny, mind you. But he lay down on the floor at the top of the stairs with me and Cameron and waited for the fun to begin. I made sure that I was in the middle, for Nerdstrom's sake. I didn't want Cameron making him squeal and giving us away.

Of course the ladies didn't get down to looking at the products straight away. Guys would. Guys would go, "So, where's this facial cleanser you've been yapping on about?" All I could hear was female voices saying, "I just *love* what you've done with the kitchen" and "It's a lovely street" and "This is gorgeous dip, Julianne!" and all that rubbish.

And me and Cameron were just like, "Come *on,* look at the face stuff," under our breath. Nerdstrom didn't say anything. Maybe he was scared. But none of the ladies were going near the face stuff, and I was starting to feel guilty and sick inside as I thought about what we'd done.

Then something happened that made me stop feeling guilty. One of the ladies said to Mum, "Julianne, this cheesecake is beautiful. Did you make it?"

That was when Mum said, "There's a funny story about that cheesecake. Did I tell you about it? No? Well, a couple of weeks ago Max's class went on an excursion to the Auntie Shirley's Kitchen factory."

And all the other ladies made noises like "Oh!" and "Really!" and "Lucky devils!" and that kind of thing.

Mum kept going, even though it would have been very easy for her to stop right there. She said, "The thing is, I gave Max some money to buy a couple of cheesecakes from the factory outlet shop." Then she went on to describe the entire incident, complete with all these details that she couldn't possibly have known, since she wasn't even there, like how much cake me and Jared ate, and how sick we got, and how our faces went green because we felt so sick, and how I threw up. And when she talked about that she even did a little impression of what I sounded like when I vomited. The ladies were laughing and begging her to stop, and the whole time I was thinking how I wasn't even slightly sorry about the satay sauce in the face cream tube anymore.

I looked at Nerdstrom. His face was blank, but Cameron was cracking up, so I got him back for the punch in the chest he'd given me before. I think I might have hurt him quite a lot, because his face began to go purple and I thought he wasn't going to be able to breathe. But I reckon he totally deserved it, and from the look he gave me once he started breathing I think he knew it.

So finally Mum finished her really hilarious story and said, "Okay everyone, let's take a look at some of these wonderful products I've got for you. I'll just put them out on the coffee table and I'll tell you about them one at a time." And that was when Cameron kind of giggled, which meant that not only had he got his breath back after I punched him in the chest, but he was also about to ruin everything. I threatened to punch him again, and he stopped, because even though he's older than me, he's also more frightened of me than I am of him.

Mum started going on about some of the different products, and if I hadn't known that something heaps funny was about to happen I would have probably gone to sleep. It was so boring, with all the stuff about how this one moisturizes without causing your skin to go all pimply, and this one here is really good when you aren't getting enough walnuts in your diet, and this one is good for vegetarians because it hasn't been tested on rabbits, even though I can't think why you'd want to remove all the fur from a rabbit's armpits to begin with. Even though I was as bored as anything, I could tell that Mum was doing a pretty good job, with the other ladies asking questions and making all sorts of agreeing kinds of noises.

Then Mum asked, "So who'd like to try this one? It's the avocado and palm oil facial scrub."

One of the ladies went, "Oh yes, I'll give that one a go." Me and Cameron held our breath. Then we heard the lady say, "It's got an interesting fragrance, Julianne."

"Yes, it's the palm oil, I believe," Mum said.

But the lady said, "It actually smells more like garlic."

Mum sounded confused then. "It shouldn't smell like garlic. Let me have a smell . . . Yes, you're right. I hadn't noticed that before."

Then someone else said, "What's this one, Julianne?"

"Oh, that's the facemask. Would you like to try it, Kate?"

Me and Cameron held our breath again. It wasn't long before the Kate person said, "Is this meant to be jojoba? It smells like something else."

Mum said, in a voice that was starting to sound stretched, "What does it smell like, Kate?"

"It actually smells like peanut butter or something, but it couldn't be . . . could it?"

Then someone else said, "This perfume—"

And Mum kind of snapped, "It's an eau de toilette, actually."

"Well, whatever it is, it's very unusual."

Someone else must have sniffed it too, because a voice said, "It actually smells quite a lot like beer."

And that was it. I heard Cameron kind of wheeze, like he was about to explode, and I couldn't hold it in another second, and we both spluttered as we tried not to laugh. And that was when we heard Mum go, "Boys?"

We could hear her footsteps coming across the floor toward the bottom of the stairs, and we jumped up and tried to escape back to Cameron's room, but we weren't fast enough. We got as far as the bedroom door and turned around, and Nerdstrom was there at the top of the stairs, right next to Mum, looking like he didn't know where he should be standing.

Man, did she give it to us! Right there in the hallway, while Nerdstrom stood quietly to one side. She wasn't shouting or anything, but she was angrier than I could ever remember her being, with her face going quite a few colors I didn't know faces could go. She told us off for ages, and would have kept going if one of the ladies hadn't come up the stairs and cleared her throat and said, "Uh, excuse me, Julianne, but where's your phone? I think we need to call an ambulance."

"What for?"

"It's for Grace. That skin toner—does it have peanuts in it?"

And Mum said, kind of impatient and cranky with this woman, "Why would it have peanuts in it?"

"Well Grace has put some on, and her face is all swollen up, and she's finding it hard to swallow. And the only thing that makes her do that is peanuts. You know, peanut butter, satay sauce, that kind of thing . . ."

I don't remember much after that except for the ambulance coming to our house and the ambulance guys giving the lady with the puffy face and fish-lips an injection and loading her into the back of the ambulance and driving off with the lights flashing. All the other ladies said goodbye to Mum, and Nerdstrom and his mum left, and Mum came back up the stairs with her lips so tight that her mouth was just a thin line, plus she had tears in her eyes. And her voice was so stretched that I thought it was going to snap like an old rusty guitar string.

I actually felt pretty bad. Very bad. But I'm learning that sometimes people get so mad that they don't say it's okay even when you say sorry and really mean it.

They just say, "It's all too late, boys. It's all far too late for that. I wish you'd known how much I needed this, and I tried to tell you, but you wouldn't listen."

Yeah, I guess I felt pretty bad. Especially when I thought about what Dad was going to do when he got back from his Army Reserve weekend.

21 DAD RUNS OUT OF IDEAS

When Dad finally did get home at about nine o'clock that Sunday night, he said that he didn't know what he was going to do with us, which I thought was a weird thing to say. I mean, usually people don't admit that they don't know what to do next. Imagine if the ambulance people who came to pick up the fish-lips lady had gone, "Oh, I don't know what to do with her or her puffy lips." She might have died, if what Dad told us was true.

Once this writer guy came to our school and said that it was heaps easy to get ideas for stories, and if you couldn't find an idea anywhere then your brain must have actually stopped working altogether. So that might be what happened to Dad, because he said, "Boys, I've run out of ideas. I don't know what I'm going to do with you, I really don't. This could have been life-threatening for poor Grace." Which probably would have been helpful to know beforehand.

There's not much point telling us that satay sauce is going to make someone's face swell up *after* it's happened. It would be much more useful to know that kind of thing *before* it happens. Because if we'd known that before, we never would have done it. Obviously.

So anyway, Dad said, "I don't know what to do with you anymore, but I am going to think of something." I was quite anxious about what it was going to be. Especially when he was wearing his Army Reserve stuff, and that uniform looks very convincing when someone's trying to scare you.

22 NERDSTROM CALLS

That Monday I got a very strange phone call. It was Nerdstrom, so getting a call from him was weird to begin with. I mean, despite what he said, I think he was frightened of me, and the only reason he didn't quiver and shake in the library when he was supposed to be helping me with my math was because he knew the librarian was there to protect him. So it was something of a surprise when he rang.

Of course, it *would* have to be Cameron who took the call. He was practically gloating when he came into my room with the phone and said, "Hey, guess who it is? It's that loser, T'riffic Triffin Nerdstrom."

I whispered, "Cameron, at least stick your hand over the phone—he can hear you!"

But Cameron just shrugged, which is kind of his default response.

I took the phone, but Nerdstrom didn't say anything about hearing what Cameron had said. He just went, "Hey, I've been thinking."

"About what?"

"About the math thing."

"Let me guess—you don't want to do it anymore."

He almost laughed, right there on the phone, and said, "I *never* wanted to do it. Our parents worked it out together, remember? I'm just doing it to keep Ulrika happy, not because I'm enjoying it one bit."

"Not even a tiny bit?" After all, most of the time he just lounged around with his book, telling me not to disturb him.

"No, not one single bit. I'm not enjoying it, but I'm not scared by it either. I'm just *doing* it."

"So what did you call me for?" I tried to sound like I thought he was really out of line calling me at home in the first place.

"I think we should try to meet somewhere else, instead of doing the tutoring at school."

"Why?"

"Because people are going to start talking."

"So what's the problem with that?" I asked. "I'm the one that everyone thinks is stupid."

He didn't say anything for a while then, for so long in fact that I had to say, "Are you still there, Nerdstrom?"

I heard him sigh. "That's the kind of thing I'm talking about, Max. When you call me Nerdstrom you're making fun of me because I'm smart. You think it's tough being stupid? Try being this person that everyone thinks is a walking brain, which I'm not. It's just that I *get* some stuff, like math and science. Besides, I don't think you're as stupid as you think you are."

"I *don't* think I'm stupid," I said. "It's just that other people do because some guy in my class who just happens to wear glasses is teaching me math twice a week."

"Exactly. Which is why we should do this out of school. During our weekend visit things, maybe."

And that was when it got weird, because I suddenly had this problem. See, I still hated Nerdstrom, even after I knew that he wasn't getting much enjoyment out of this tutoring thing. Why did I hate him? Because if it wasn't for him taking the whole cake factory incident so personally, none of this stuff would have been happening. So I had this decision to make. If we kept doing the tutoring in the library at school, who would suffer more—him or me? Who would get more embarrassed—me being the dummy, or him being the nerdy brainhead?

I decided that I'd do what I thought was the right thing. After all, there was my reputation to think of. If anyone decided to pick on me I'd just remind them of that, and they'd probably stop. But what did Nerdstrom have? A weird name and an unhealthy interest in fat, geeky wizard books. That, and a term of sneaking out of the library for fear of being called The Professor.

"I don't think we should mix business and pleasure," I said. "We'll keep doing it at school."

23 LOYAL CASEY

That Tuesday I had a meat pie for lunch and it was nice. It was especially nice because of the way I got it.

The thing is, I lost my lunch money again. Cameron goes to Red Hill High, and they have this awesome school cafeteria, and I think that sometimes he pinches my lunch money from my bag so he can buy more stuff. I haven't been able to prove it, but there might be a way I could set up some kind of surveillance thing to watch my bag. That would require a video camera, which we have, except Dad won't let me use it anymore. I mean, you'd think that masking tape would be strong enough to hold a video camera on a radio-controlled monster truck, but Mum had bought the masking tape from one of those junky bargain-bin shops that are filled to the ceiling with photo frames, plastic kitchen stuff, and cheap batteries. So the masking tape cost only a dollar a roll, and it wouldn't grip onto the camera very well. So after that Dad wouldn't let me use the new video camera either, which he kept locked in the filing cabinet in his office.

Anyway, when the time came for me to go to the canteen to buy my lunch, there was no money to spend. I thought about asking Jared for some of his lunch, but he likes his food too much and he never would have agreed. He might have given me a bite of his muesli bar or something, but that's not going to fill up a growing boy like me.

Then I saw Casey, and decided it was time to make him earn his recruit stripes. I mean, it'd been heaps of fun up until then, with the tipping over of the drinks and the flicking up of girls' skirts with rulers and all the other funny stuff we made him do, but I decided that the time was right to make him *really* earn them. There were about three or four other first graders following Casey around, which was kind of cool, the way he'd made his own little posse, and I was actually quite proud to see how well he was using the leadership skills I was teaching him.

I called him over and he came straight away, because he was always good like that. And I said, "Hi, Casey, I've got a job for you. But you've got to get rid of these others."

So Casey turned to his posse and said, "I've got to talk to Max Quigley."

The little kids were looking up at me and Jared all awestruck, but they didn't move, so Jared had to step in and say, "Go on, get lost, you little slobberers."

The little slobberers took off, and Casey said, "Why did they have to go, Max?"

"Because I've got a job for you," I said again. "And I don't want them all telling on you. You've got to do this mission alone."

And Casey looked excited and scared, both at once. But I knew he'd be fine, because he's a brave little kid. "What do you want me to do?" he asked.

"You know Mr. French?" I said, and Casey nodded, and looked a little more scared.

"Yeah, I know him," Casey said. "He's the one who's a shouting teacher."

"That's the guy," I said. "And every lunchtime he goes and buys a pie from the canteen."

Casey didn't say anything. He was still listening to me, which was one of the things I liked about him.

"And when he gets his pie, he goes back to his classroom and puts it on his desk. Then he goes over to the staffroom and gets a cup of coffee and the newspaper. Then he goes back to his classroom to read the paper and eat his lunch. You keeping up with me?"

"Yeah, I'm keeping up," Casey said.

"Good. So when he comes past, I want you to follow him. Then when he puts his pie on the desk and goes over to the staffroom, I want you to grab it."

For a minute it seemed like Casey totally wasn't going to do it. He just looked around, as if he were making sure that no one had heard what we were saying. Then he said, "But that's stealing, Max."

Me and Jared didn't say anything. I thought about telling Casey that it wasn't stealing, but I thought that if I said that, I'd find it really hard to say what it was instead. So I didn't say anything at all.

"It's stealing," Casey repeated.

"Yeah, and Max is hungry," Jared said. "So you'll do it, all right?"

Then Casey said something that was slightly stupid but very brave. He said to me, "Hey Max, if you're so hungry, why don't *you* steal his pie?"

And that was when Jared leaned down and put his face close to Casey's and said, "Because if he gets caught, he gets a detention, and maybe even gets suspended. But if *you* get caught, you just get some teacher telling you that stealing is wrong. And you can just go, 'Sorry, I didn't know it was stealing.' Okay? Because you're in first grade, okay?"

"That's right," I said. "Plus, I'll give you a pack of gum if you do it."

"Really?" said Casey.

"Yup. I've got one in my pocket."

Casey's eyes were huge. "Where do you get gum from? They don't sell candy at the canteen."

As if I didn't know that! "I buy them on the way to school," I said. "Here comes Mr. French now, so off you go. If you're quick, you won't get caught anyway. But you'll have to be quick, because the staffroom's right next to his classroom. He's only gone for a couple of minutes."

Casey looked over at Mr. French, who was walking toward us. Me and Jared turned our backs as he got closer, because if Casey did get caught we didn't want Mr. French to automatically assume we were involved just because he'd seen us talking to Casey.

"Go on," I whispered. "And good luck."

Casey did exactly the right thing. He didn't argue anymore or anything. He just followed Mr. French around the end of the building, walking a safe distance behind.

A couple of minutes later he was back, carrying a

TARGET
LOCKED ON.
(PIE, MEAT)

brown paper bag. He looked sort of triumphant or something, like he'd just convinced his parents to let him have ice cream for breakfast every day for the rest of the year. He handed me the bag. "There you go, Max. There's your pie."

"Good for you," I said, checking in the bag. Yes, it was a pie. I took it out and handed Casey the empty bag. "Get rid of that for me," I said, and just like always, Casey did exactly what I said, walking to the nearest garbage can and dropping it in.

Then he was back, standing there and looking up

at me like a puppy waiting for a treat. "What now?" I said.

"You said you'd give me something."

"Yeah, a smack if you don't get lost," Jared said, but that wasn't it at all.

I put my hand in my pocket and took out a pack of gum. "There you go," I said, handing it to Casey.

"Cool! Thanks, Max!" Casey said. Then he turned and scampered off as fast as he could.

"Where's mine?" asked Jared, in a whiny kind of voice. "You give that little weed some chewy, but what about me, your best mate?"

I shook my head. "You didn't get me a pie, did you?"

"But I would have, if you'd asked," he said.

"Nah, I doubt it," I replied, and I started eating the pie. It was delicious.

24 NERDSTROM HAS A THEORY

That Wednesday me and Nerdstrom went for our usual math session in the library. We'd only done it a couple of times, but it was starting to get easier, and every time I asked him a math question it didn't feel like I had to persuade him to help me, and there wasn't all that weirdness about asking someone my own age for help. Yes, it was strange, but so was Nerdstrom.

He'd finished reading his big fat fantasy book and had started another. I said, "When did you finish that other one?" and he just shrugged.

"The other day. I read heaps of books. I like it."

"Why?" I asked.

"Why do you like picking on people?" he asked me.

I waited, in case it was a rhetorical question, and if it was, he'd tell me the answer. But it wasn't, so he didn't. So finally I had to answer his question. I said, "I don't."

Nerdstrom totally laughed at me, which I couldn't remember him doing before. He said, "Yes you do. You do it all the time."

"Like when?"

Nerdstrom thought for a minute. "What about the time you took that kid's basketball and threw it over the fence into the dam?"

That was easy. "He was bouncing it near me, and I told him not to, heaps of times," I said. "So it was his fault anyway. He could have walked away."

"What about when you tipped all the books out of Wendy Fowler's bag at the bus stop?"

"She poked her tongue out at me," I said. "And anyway, that was last year, so that doesn't count."

"What about when you locked me out of the cake factory?"

That was easy too. "Your fault," I said.

He looked confused. "How was that my fault?"

"You were tattling on about how much of the free food me and Jared ate," I explained. "You got what you deserved. Anyway, that door had a big red warning sign on it. Totally your fault."

And Nerdstrom said, "Yes, but you *pushed* me out."

"You could have shouted," I said.

He seemed disappointed that I'd thought of an answer. "Yeah, I guess I could have shouted," he said, sounding kind of deflated. "But you know what? It wasn't me who told on you."

"Who was it then?" I asked. "I remember you talking to Sigsy just before he got us in trouble about going back more than once."

"I was asking him which cake was his favorite," said Nerdstrom. "That's all. I think he said he liked the ginger cheesecake best."

Just then Mrs. Lalor came over, and she was looking mean and cranky, which is nothing new for her. She said, "Are you boys here to work or to talk?"

And I thought about saying, "To talk, actually," but something stopped me. I'm not sure what it was. Maybe it was the EXIT sign above the library door, except I don't know why that would have made me stop. But whatever the reason was, I just said, "Sorry, Mrs. Lalor. We're here to do work."

Then she said, still grumpy for some reason, "So get on with it, will you?" which was quite rude really.

When the bell rang for the end of school, Nerdstrom and I stood up. "It's all right, I'll go first," he said, sighing, and he started toward the door. I thought about following after him so we could leave the library together, but there were already a lot of sixth grade kids out the front of the library, so I let him go. There was a new magazine on the rack that I wanted to look at anyway.

Then Jared came in. "How did your lesson go?" he asked, and I gave him a dirty look.

I said, "You're lucky that you're not in here with the Prof as well. He's so awful, and he's like 'Keep working or I'll tell Sigsy how stupid you are' and all that stuff. Can you believe he calls him Sigsy? That's totally our thing—yours and mine." I jammed the magazine back into the rack. "Come on, let's go."

Jared pulled the magazine back out and read the front cover. "You don't like bushwalking."

"Yeah I do."

"Since when?"

"Since I heard about this guy who got his arm trapped under this rock and had to cut it off," I said.

And Jared went, "His own arm? No way! Really?"

"Totally," I said. "Right off, with a pocketknife."

"That's so cool!"

We went out the front of the library. There were

kids all over the place, mostly little ones, screaming and running and chasing each other and trying to carry bags and projects and crafts as they headed for the buses and cars.

"Hey, Max," said this weedy little voice. It was Casey, with his posse. "Guess what, Max?"

"What?"

"I'm having tennis lessons. I started yesterday."

"So what?" said Jared.

"Cool," I said.

But Casey wasn't finished. "Yeah, and guess who my tennis teacher is? It's Mrs. Sigsworth. You know, Sigsy's wife! Cool, hey?"

I heard Jared grunt. Then he said, sort of under

his breath, "Sigsy, huh? *Our* thing, huh? Yeah, right."

I looked at Jared. "What's your problem?" I asked.

But he just said, "There's no problem, dude, no problem at all. I'll see you tomorrow, Max."

25 JARED GETS SICK AND TIRED

That Friday Jared wasn't at school. It was kind of lonely, I guess, but I'd never tell him that. I'm pretty sure that he thinks I mope around all pathetic and sad when he's not there, but I don't. I mean, I like having my best friend around, but it's not like my world comes all crashing down when he's not there.

I rang him up as soon as I got home. He sounded heaps sick, and all croaky.

"Are you all right?" I asked him.

He said, "Do I sound all right?"

I suppose he didn't. "So when are you coming back to school?" I asked him.

"I dunno," he said. "My mum thinks I'll be okay for Monday, so we'll see."

"So what did you do all day?" I asked. "How many DVDs did you watch?"

He didn't answer for a bit, because he was coughing so hard I thought he might actually launch one of his lungs down the phone line at me. When he'd stopped coughing, he said, "I didn't watch many movies at all. I was just sleeping, mostly."

"Are you serious?" I said, because the way I saw it, being away from school but not able to watch movies was such a wasted opportunity.

Then Jared said, "Did you have math stuff with Nerdstrom today?"

And I didn't really want to talk about it, so I just said, "Yeah, and it was fine. But something else happened that was totally awesome. Casey did this thing—"

"Who?" Jared said. "Oh, yeah, him. What did the Boy Wonder do this time? Save you from certain death? Steal a sports car for you to drive home in? Find you a—" But he didn't finish that sentence because he was coughing again.

"No, nothing like that," I said. "Mrs. Ween went to sleep in the library when she was supposed to be watching all the first graders doing computer stuff, and me and Nerdstrom were in there doing our math, and we dared Casey to climb under the desk and tie her shoelaces together. Because you know how she wears those big clumpy shoes—"

"*We* dared him. As in you and Nerdstrom?" said Jared.

"Well, no, just me really. But you know how she wears those clumpy shoes?"

"Yeah, I know the ones. That's heaps funny," Jared said, but he didn't sound like he thought it was very funny at all. "Did you give him a pack of gum for doing that?"

I frowned, and said, "No, it was just a dare. Why would I give him gum for doing a dare?"

"I guess you wouldn't. You know what, I have to go. I think I need to go back to bed."

And he hung up before I could even tell him how Mrs. Ween had almost fallen over.

Then I started wondering whether Cameron had any candy hidden away in his room.

26 THE TREB

That Saturday it was my turn to go to Nerdstrom's house. Of course I tried to convince Mum and Dad that these sessions weren't going to fix anything, and that there wasn't anything to fix anyway, and that I should be able to stay home. But they're pretty stubborn, my parents, and at about a quarter past nine, Mum said, "Okay, Max, it's time to go."

I sighed and followed Mum out to the car. "Ulrika's going to bring you home afterwards," she told me.

"When?" I asked, and she just smiled.

"Afterwards," she repeated. "Later."

While we were driving, Mum asked me how it was going with Nerdstrom.

"Fine, I guess," I said. "He's pretty weird though, Mum. He doesn't say much."

"Maybe he thinks you're weird too," she said, and I should have known that's what she'd say. Mum likes to look at things that way. She's right into this whole "Treat people how you'd like to be treated" thing, which is fine, I suppose, but it's not really that simple. I mean, Cameron told me about these nut-jobs who like to get spikes stuck through their eyebrows and stuff. That's how they like to be treated, but I wouldn't want them to start treating *me* like that. So that rule stops working straight away, doesn't it? So like I say, it's really not that simple.

So I just nodded and said, "I guess he's okay. But I still don't see why I can't pick my own friends."

She ignored this, which is a really annoying habit she has, where if she can't think of an answer she acts like she hasn't heard the question. Instead she went, "Mr. Sigsworth says your math is improving. Triffin must be really helping you."

I wanted to tell her that it had nothing to do with Nerdstrom, and that I was only working harder so I could stop going to the library twice a week to do math, but I decided not to say anything. As long as my parents and Mr. Sigsworth believed that my math was getting better, the more likely it was that all the tutoring rubbish could stop. And that was what I wanted more than anything.

So I just said, "Yeah, it's fine, I guess. Even though I didn't think my math was all that bad to begin with."

Then Mum gave me this sideways look and chuckled.

As we pulled up in the front of the Nordstroms' little house in the bush, Mum opened her door, took a deep breath, and said, "Oh, I wish I lived out here in a place like this."

And I said, "Why? It's in the *bush*."

"I know, Max, but that's why I love it. It's so peaceful."

I opened my door. All I could hear was the sound of birds, screaming like their feathers were being yanked out by the handful. "It's not *that* peaceful," I said. "Hear that? Listen. Listen."

"Oh Max," she said. "Come on, quit stalling. This is good for you."

Yeah, I thought, in the same way that having a leg cut off is good for you, but only if you have gangrene. But I didn't say it.

Mum rang the cowbell beside the door and Nerdstrom opened up almost straight away.

"Hello, Triffin," said Mum.

He said, "Hi," and then called out, "Ulrika, they're here."

I heard his mum call from somewhere near the back of the house. "Very good, Triffin. So invite them in, dear. Don't leave them out on the step."

"Would you like to come in?" Nerdstrom said, taking a step backwards into the house and holding the door open for us.

Their house still smelled weird to me. Not horribly weird, just kind of perfumy. Me and Mum sat down side by side on the couch, with its bright cushions and rugs, and I guess we looked nervous, maybe. But we didn't have to feel that way for very long, because Nerdstrom's mum came in a minute later. She was wearing a big long flowing skirt and like always she had bare feet, which were kind of dirty, like she'd been walking around in the garden without any shoes on.

We stood up as she came in, and she walked straight over and gave Mum a big hug. Then she turned to me and looked like she was going to give me one as well. But I just stuck my hand out, which I think might have been a relief for Nerdstrom, who was standing nearby looking kind of terrified.

"Hello, Max," Nerdstrom's mum said.

And I said, "Hello, Mrs. Nordstrom."

She laughed and said, in a voice that got suddenly quite serious, "Listen to me, Max. You're *not* to call me that anymore, do you understand? You're not. You're to call me Ulrika? Yes?"

I felt myself smile, even though I didn't mean to. "All right," I said. "Ulrika."

Then she grinned this huge grin, and I saw how white her teeth were, and she clapped her hands. "Excellent!" she said. "Sit back down, and I'll make some tea. Triffin, remember what we talked about?"

And Nerdstrom said, in a tired, weak kind of voice, "Would you like to see my room?"

"Yeah, okay, I guess," I said.

And from the look on my mum's face, you'd think I'd just said something wonderful and thrilling.

So I followed Nerdstrom to his room, which was possibly the strangest room I'd ever seen. There was a really high wall on one side, made out of this stuff that looked like dried mud, and there was a platform built against it, with a ladder going up to it, and I guessed that must have been where Nerdstrom's bed was. And that was pretty cool, actually.

The wall opposite the dried mud one was all glass, with bush outside, and this big glass sliding door that led out to a kind of porch thing that had no railings. Under the platform where the bed was, there was a desk, with books and stuff all over it, and a bookcase as tall as me, full of those fat fantasy books Nerdstrom likes. In one corner, on a huge mat, were more Legos than I've ever seen. Most were in a big pile, but some had been sorted into smaller piles, and there were a few models half-built. There was a Roman ship with all the slaves and oars, and a bridge, and this huge thing that might have been a crane or something.

I used to play with Legos, but I hadn't for ages. I thought about saying something mean about Nerdstrom playing with Legos, but then I thought that if I did that, I wouldn't be able to play with them when I got bored later and decided that's what I wanted to do. So instead I just went, "Legos. You've got heaps, huh?"

Nerdstrom looked kind of embarrassed, and he said, "I like to relax with it sometimes, which is childish, I guess. But I like it . . . You won't tell anyone, will you?" But the look on his face kind of told me that he knew that I could never keep a promise like that. So he shrugged and said, "Whatever. It's just Legos."

"Legos are cool," I said.

And Nerdstrom said, "Really? You think so?"

"Sure," I said. Then I started looking for Nerdstrom's TV, because as well as having to mow lawns and wash cars, dishes, and the dog for the next five hundred years, I'd had my TV privileges taken away for even longer after the Natureway party, and I was really missing it. "Where's your TV?" I asked.

"I don't have one," Nerdstrom said. "*We* don't have one."

I couldn't believe this. "Not even one? In the whole house? They're heaps cheap to buy now. Your mum could get a little one for a hundred bucks, maybe even less."

Nerdstrom laughed. "No, we don't have a TV because we don't *want* a TV."

"Really?"

"Really. Except sometimes I wish we did. But Ulrika says . . . never mind. We don't have one . . . So, do you want to do some math?"

"No! No way, I'm not . . . oh, you're not serious."

Nerdstrom was actually laughing at me. I could hardly believe it. Him, laughing at me!

"Not funny," I said.

"Sorry," he said, but I don't think he was.

I turned around and looked at his room some

more. As well as the Legos, he had a few models and things on his bookcase, and some posters of stars and planets and other predictably nerdy stuff. Plus he had a telescope over by one of the windows.

I said, "I used to have one of those, but Cameron broke it."

And Nerdstrom just went, "Imagine my surprise."

Then I said, "You know what, Nerdstrom? I totally expected that you'd have *Star Wars* stuff all over the place."

He shook his head. "I'm not really into that sort of thing. And I don't dress up like a Klingon either, before you say that."

"I wasn't going to say that," I said, and I really wasn't. "You know what? This room is actually kind of cool. Except it totally needs a TV, but never mind. Apart from that I kind of like it, especially the upstairs bed thing. So what *is* that thing, anyway?" I pointed at the crane thing made out of Legos. It was almost as tall as me, with a gray frame holding up a long black beam, which was held into the frame by a kind of axle deal. A container about the size of a box of tissues was hanging from the short end of the beam, also made from Legos. And the whole thing rested on four big black wheels.

Nerdstrom didn't answer, so I asked him again. "Nerdstrom, what's this thing?" I poked it with my finger, and the beam rocked a little.

"You're going to think I'm such a dweeb," he said.

"I already do," I replied.

"It's . . . it's a treb."

"A what?"

"A treb. A trebuchet."

"What, like a catapult thing?"

He said, "Yeah, a medieval instrument of war. A siege machine."

"Does it work?"

He almost sounded offended, "Yeah, it works. It'll throw a golf ball fifty meters or so."

"No way!" I said. "Really?"

"Sure." Then he said, in a kind of hopeful voice, "I can show you if you like."

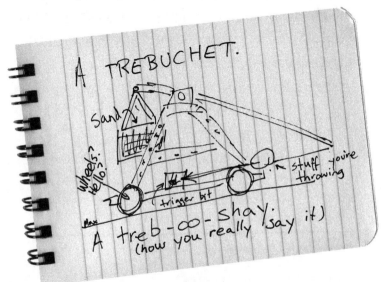

I suddenly had a thought. If I did something really nerdy like firing a golf ball with a trebuchet that was made out of Legos, would that make me a nerd like Triffin Nordstrom, or just someone researching nerd behavior? Then I decided that it would only make me a nerd if I actually enjoyed it.

So, totally determined *not* to enjoy it, I said, "Yeah, well since you don't have a PlayStation or even a TV, I guess we'll have to do that instead."

Nerdstrom went over to the sliding door and opened it. "We'll take it out there," he said. "It's safer outside."

"Really? Safer?"

Nerdstrom smiled. "Treb plus golf ball plus window equals glass divided by about a million."

"No math today, remember?"

Once we got the treb out onto the porch, he said, "Just hang on a minute—I've got to get the counterweight." And he jumped down off the porch and disappeared around the end of the house.

I heard the bedroom door open, and Mum put her head in. She smiled when she saw me. "Where's Triffin?"

And I thought about saying, "I don't know. He's

been totally ignoring me, so you might as well take me home." But I didn't. I just said, "He's gone to get something."

Mum smiled some more, and told me for about the twentieth time that Ulrika would take me home. Then she told me to have fun, as if she'd forgotten that this was meant to be some kind of cruel punishment.

"Yeah, fine," I said, keen for her to leave the room before Nerdstrom came back. "See you."

And she closed the door.

Nerdstrom was back a minute or two later, with a small bucket of sand. "This is it," he said. "The counterweight."

"Sand?"

"Yep. It's nice and dense, which makes it heavy, especially when it's damp."

"What are the wheels for?" I asked, while he poured the sand into the container and dug around in one of his drawers for a golf ball.

And then I wished I hadn't asked, because Nerdstrom started talking about how if a catapult is on wheels it soaks up the vibration or something, and how the ones with wheels throw heaps farther than

the ones without, which seemed all back to front to me, because things that have wheels move and things that don't don't. When he started drawing a diagram for me I just went, "Whatever. Can we just like fire this thing?" Even though he was a heaps good drawer.

So Nerdstrom finished loading the treb, and he showed me how to do it and everything, and then we had it all pulled back and ready to go. "Are you sure this is going to work?" I asked.

"Yeah, of course." Then he handed me the string that was hooked up to the trigger bit, and he said,

"Would you like to do the honors? You just have to give it a good yank."

That was pretty good of him, I thought, so I said I would. Then I took the string in my hand, he counted down from three, and I pulled the string, hard.

Man, that thing was awesome! It reminded me of this video I saw once of a cobra striking a mouse or something, and it was all kind of tight and stretched, then *whang!* it struck. And the treb was like that. It flung its arm around and up, and the golf ball flew around in its little sling, then it was suddenly disappearing into the bush. There was a loud *clock* off among the trees somewhere, and the treb was just sitting there, its arm pointing straight up and rocking slightly.

I looked at Nerdstrom. He seemed very proud, and I had to admit that I was pretty impressed too. "Did you build this yourself?" I asked him.

"Yeah, of course. It's my own design. Do you like it?"

"It's okay."

"Do you want to fire something else?"

"If you like," I said. "Like what?"

"Rocks. Other stuff." He smiled, which was something I hadn't seen him do very much. "Ulrika's veggie rissoles, for example. They'd bring down a small castle on their own."

Ulrika took me home in the orange Volvo straight after we'd had lunch. She'd made us salad sandwiches on this dark brown bread, which looked awful but tasted all right. And I didn't have to drink evil green juice, because we just had water.

Nerdstrom didn't come with us, because he had to stay at home and do some jobs for his mum. I thought that it would feel awkward, being in the car with just this strange hippie woman, but it wasn't as bad as I'd expected. I mean, she talked a lot. A real lot. But she was nice, I decided.

When we were almost at our place, she said, "Max, I want to say thanks for agreeing to spend some time with Triffin."

And I said, "That's okay," even though that felt like a lie, after all the times I'd tried to get out of it.

And she said, "Julianne tells me that your math is coming along quite well."

For a second I had to think about who Julianne was. "Yeah, it's okay, I guess," I said.

"There was another reason why we thought this

would be a good idea. You might have noticed that Triffin is very shy. Painfully shy."

I'd noticed this, of course, so I just nodded.

"You see, Max, you're different. You're a very confident young man, and I was really hoping that you could help Triffin find himself."

If he goes and loses himself, there's not a lot I can do, I thought. But what I actually said was, "What do you mean, exactly?"

She shook her head and smiled. "It's nothing specific, Max. Just . . . I just want him to be confident. Like you are, I suppose."

We were pulling up in front of my house by then, which I was pretty happy about, since this conversation was getting weirder by the second.

"I'll do what I can," I said as I got out. "See you later, Ulrika."

"Goodbye, Max. See you next time."

And when I thought about it, I decided that it hadn't been such an awful day.

27 JARED KIND OF FINDS OUT

I hadn't told Jared that I was spending every weekend with Nerdstrom, but that Monday he kind of found out. I was actually being really careful, because I didn't want to go blurting about the trebuchet or anything, even though I'd thought about it heaps and had even started drawing a few designs in my homework diary for one of my own. But I wasn't going to say, "Hey, guess what, Jared! Nerdstrom's got a trebuchet in his bedroom," because the next question he'd ask would be how I could know such a thing, and then it would get peculiar and actually quite ugly. So I wasn't going to say anything.

But I didn't have to, because when me and Jared were putting our bags on our hooks, Nerdstrom turned up as well.

And he went, "Max."

And I went, "Nerdstrom."

Just then a tennis ball came bouncing over from a

game of handball that some kids were playing nearby, and Nerdstrom picked it up. He held it and looked at it for a bit, then he said to me, "How do you reckon our treb would go with one of these?"

He threw the ball back to the handballers then, and I don't think he even realized what he'd done until he glanced our way and saw that I had this blank look on my face, and that Jared was wearing a puzzled frown.

Nerdstrom tried to fix his mistake, which was good. He said, "But I guess you wouldn't know what I'm talking about, would you? It's just that me and my friend have just got this thing . . . this really nerdy thing that we made."

"A treb?" said Jared. "As in a trebuchet?"

Then I said, surprised and maybe a little too excited, "Yeah. Do you know about trebuchets?"

And Jared started looking back and forth between me and Nerdstrom, and I think if I'd listened really closely I might have heard the cogs in his brain clicking around. Then he asked, "What's going on?"

"Nothing's going on," I said.

"Really?"

"Yeah, totally," I said. "What could be going on?" Then I laughed. "Do you think that me and Nerdstrom . . . Are you *serious?* Like I'd be hanging out with *him!*"

And Nerdstrom started taking his books out of his bag, and I heard him say, real quietly to himself, "Yeah, as if *that* would happen."

28 THE POEM

That Wednesday me and Nerdstrom had our usual math thing in the library. It was taking me heaps less time to get through the work, and I was really hoping that Mr. Sigsworth would soon be able to tell my parents that I didn't need to be tutored anymore.

So we were sitting there, and I was doing my math, and I glanced up at Nerdstrom, who had a folder open in front of him rather than his usual fat, dweeby fantasy book. And his lips were moving as he read from it.

"What are you reading?" I asked him.

"What? Oh, just a poem."

I tried not to laugh. "A poem? Why?"

He seemed embarrassed. "Don't worry about it," he said.

I reached across and grabbed the folder before he could react. "Let me see," I said. I started to read the poem. It was all crazy, in words I'd never seen before. "What *is* this?"

"I told you, it's a poem."

"Yeah, I know, but it's in some other language. What's a *brillig?* And what's a *borogrove?* And *manxome?* What does *manxome* mean?"

He snatched the folder back. "It's nonsense. Just forget about it."

But I wasn't satisfied with his answer so I said, "Why are you reading that stupid poem anyway? *I* could write a better poem than that. *And* I'd use real words."

Then Nerdstrom laughed, which was pretty rude, I thought. "You could write a better poem? I doubt it."

"Why do you doubt it?"

"Because 'Jabberwocky' is a classic."

I snorted then. I'd been starting to think that Nerdstrom maybe wasn't as kooky as I'd always thought he was, but now I was changing my mind back again.

"Classic?" I said. "You are a serious oddball, Nerdstrom."

"Math," he said.

29 STUPID CASEY

That Thursday Casey did something stupid. I'd started to think that he was a bright little guy who had some real promise, and then he went and did something really dumb.

Me and Jared were sitting down near the oval eating our lunch when we saw Casey wandering past at the head of his posse, which was bigger now, maybe six or seven kids, and some of them were in grades above him. He'd come along really nicely, and had turned into a good leader, I thought. I was actually kind of proud of him.

Except what he did next wasn't the kind of thing

I'd taught him to do. He walked up to us, bold as anything, and asked me, "Have you got any candy today? Any gum?"

I said, "No, not today."

And Jared went, "No, we haven't got anything for you, so get lost."

That was when Casey did something unexpected, and maybe he was showing off to all his friends, but he poked his tongue out at Jared, and said, "You shut up, you big idiot." And that would have been okay, and even funny, except that when Jared stood up really slowly and started to move toward him Casey hardly even flinched or anything. He just got this smug little smile on his face, and he said, "What are you going to do? Max is sitting right there."

So I said, "Yeah, I am, but if you're rude to us Jared can still thump you. I'll let him."

And Jared looked at me then, and he said, "I don't need you to give me permission to thump little kids."

He had a point, I suppose, but that didn't stop Casey from saying, "Yes, you do. You don't do anything without Max saying it's okay."

That cut Jared, I reckon, and he took another step toward Casey, and he said, "I'll still thump you."

I could hardly believe what Casey said next. He went, "There's heaps of us, and only two of you. Plus there are teachers all over the place."

"I'll do it when none of the teachers are around," Jared said. "Little kids don't scare me. I'll punch you good."

But Casey was *still* ahead of him. He said, "You're going to Red Hill High in a couple of years, aren't you?"

"Yeah. So?"

"And guess what? So does my brother, and Liam's brother, plus Harry's sister, and she's *real* mean. And you and Max won't be the biggest kids in the school then. So *see* you."

And they walked away.

"He thinks he's so smart," Jared muttered.

"That's because he is," I said.

30 NERDSTROM KNOWS IT

That Friday in math tutoring, Nerdstrom had his book out again. I said, "What, no poem today?"

He shook his head. "I already know it," he said.

"You know it? Really?"

"Yes. I know it by heart."

"Off you go then," I said.

"What?"

"I'm waiting. Say the poem."

But Nerdstrom shook his head. "No way. I'm not reciting it to you."

"Why not? Why did you learn it anyway?"

He shrugged, and said, "Because I like it, that's all."

"And you actually know it by heart?"

"Yep."

"You're weird."

"Math," he said.

And I said, "What's the poem called again?"

"'Jabberwocky.' It's by Lewis Carroll."

"How do you spell that?" I asked him

He frowned. "Why do you want to know?"

"Because it sounds stupid. And I like stupid words, like your last name."

"It's not stupid, but if you must know, it's spelt like this."

And while he spelt it out to me, I wrote it down on my hand.

"'Jabberwocky,'" I said, reading it. "Dumb."

"Math."

"Yeah, that's dumb too," I replied.

31 I DO SOME RESEARCH

That Saturday I got on the Internet and looked up Nerdstrom's stupid nonsense poem. It didn't take long to find. And it was full of ridiculous words I'd never even heard of, like *vorpal* and *frumious* and *frabjous* and *gimble,* and I started thinking that it would be heaps easier to remember it if it had real words in it.

But later on I found that I couldn't get the first line of Nerdstrom's poem out of my head. "'Twas brillig, and the slithy toves did gyre and gimble in the wabe,'" I was muttering to myself, and Cameron stopped in my bedroom doorway, on his way back from the kitchen with two slices of bread and honey and a glass of milk.

"What was that you were saying?" he asked me.

"Nothing," I said.

But he wasn't going to be put off that easily. "Don't tell me it's nothing. You were saying something."

"It's just nonsense," I said.

"Like everything else you say," Cameron replied as he wandered off to his own room.

But that line was stuck in my head, so I went back online and printed off the poem. It was kind of cool, I decided, after reading it through a couple of times.

But one thing was for sure. I wasn't going to tell Nerdstrom that I'd read it all the way through. And I *definitely* wasn't going to tell him that I'd read it all the way through a couple of times.

32 NERDSTROM REFUSES TO HELP HIMSELF

That Sunday Nerdstrom came to our place again. Cameron was down at the skate park with some of his friends, which was a relief, because I didn't feel like having him there making fun of me and Nerdstrom doing whatever we were going to do.

Before Nerdstrom arrived, Mum was reading the Sunday paper at the kitchen table, and when I asked her what I should do with Nerdstrom, she shook her head at me and frowned. "I do wish you wouldn't call him that."

"What, Nerdstrom?"

"Yes, that. It's an awful thing to call someone. What if someone gave you a nickname?"

"I wouldn't mind."

"I think you would mind, if it was a horrible, disrespectful nickname like Nerdstrom. Why don't you call him by the name his parents gave him?"

And I said, "I don't know, Mum. Maybe because Triffin is a ridiculous name."

"Well yes, maybe you're right, but it's *his* ridiculous name," Mum said. "And you should use it."

"It doesn't matter what I call him—he's still going to be bored while he's here."

Mum blinked at me. "Did you tell me that they don't have a TV?"

"That's right, no TV at all. He's not even interested. He just plays with Legos and reads books and looks at the bush. Plus he's a heaps good drawer."

"Then you should go for a walk or something," Mum suggested. "Take some pencils and paper and draw what you see."

And I looked at Mum like she had three heads.

"What?" she said. "You asked me for a suggestion."

"We're not walking anywhere, Mum. I'll be showing him how to play PlayStation . . ." I stopped and held my breath. Technically I was still banned from playing video games, so mentioning the PlayStation was a complete accident. A very stupid accident, like the kind Cameron would make.

Mum shrugged and went back to her paper. "Okay. So do that."

I breathed again. It looked like I'd gotten away with it.

And PlayStation is what we did. Nerdstrom wasn't too bad, actually, and he learned heaps fast, even though I smashed him at *Street Battle 3*. Maybe it was because I knew some of the cheats, but he didn't mind, because he didn't say anything about it, even though it was obvious that I had a few secret moves that I could keep putting on him again and again.

Then we played a couple of fantasy games, but after a while he kind of lost interest and started looking at his watch.

And I said, "That's a pretty cool watch. Where'd you get it?"

"My dad sent it to me."

"Where's your dad live?"

"Back in Sweden, where I was born," he said. "He's an artist, like Ulrika. A photographer, actually. Ulrika does pottery."

"And what's your dad's name?"

"Halsten," he said. "Halsten Nordstrom. It's Swedish, obviously. Stupid name, isn't it?"

I didn't know what to say. It wasn't the dumbest

name I'd ever heard, but it was still pretty odd. "I've heard stupider ones," I lied.

"Yeah, right. It's almost as stupid as *Triffin* Nordstrom."

So I asked him, "Have you ever thought about changing your name?"

"To what? Bob?"

"No, to something like Triff, or Finn."

He turned up his nose. "Finn? That's no good at all."

"Well it was only a suggestion, but if you don't like Triffin or Bob, then it's probably got to be Triff or Finn, doesn't it?"

Nerdstrom scratched his neck. "I don't know. I guess I can just be Triffin Nordstrom. It's who I am, after all."

Yeah, and you'll get teased all your life because of it, I thought. But that's your problem, not mine.

Then I decided that no matter how much you try to help someone, if they don't *want* to be helped, there's not much you can do.

33 WE PUT THE SMACK-DOWN ON

That Monday me and Jared worked on our routine for Literature Day. We went into the library and started looking for a book about wrestlers, because Mr. Sigsworth was being really strict about it. He'd said to the whole class, "I don't care what you do, guys, but it has to be from a book. A book, all right? You know, with paper pages and printing. So if you want to put fifteen cockroaches up your nose in a reference to that guy from the *Guinness Book of World Records,* that's fine, but it *has to be a book."*

And it was at that point that Marcus Olmstead had put his hand up and said, "How about video games?" But Marcus Olmstead eats his snot, so that was the kind of question you'd expect from him.

So me and Jared went into the library in search of a book about wrestling, and we found it in no time. It was called *A Photographic Guide to the World of Professional Wrestling,* and it was heaps full of wrestling stuff—not just the guys from the TV, but guys in black and white as well. As soon as we found that, we knew that Mr. Sigsworth wouldn't be able to argue. So I borrowed it, just so we could prove to Sigsy that we hadn't made it up.

We found a quiet corner of the playground to work on our routine, but eventually we had to go to Mr. Sigsworth and ask if we could practice in the classroom.

And he said, "Why, boys?"

I said, "Because every time we start wrestling, some teacher comes over and tells us to stop fighting."

Mr. Sigsworth said, "Well, you know, if that's what they're used to seeing, you can hardly blame them . . . okay, fine, I'll let you into the classroom. I was going to check out all the routines first anyway, so I might as well do yours now."

So we went into his classroom, and we showed him the wrestling book, which made him shake his head and chuckle. Then he sat on a desk and ate his sandwiches while we stood in front and practiced shouting insults at each other.

"And then we'll actually do a few wrestling moves, and that'll be it," I said after a while.

"And who's going to win this ferocious battle of

the brawn?" Mr. Sigsworth asked, with his mouth full.

"Oh, we haven't worked that bit out yet," I replied.

"But he'll probably say it has to be him," said Jared.

"Maybe you'll just have to toss a coin," Mr. Sigsworth suggested. "Either that or battle it out to the death. But that's fine, guys."

"Can we keep practicing in here?" I asked.

"Sure. Just lock up when you go," Mr. Sigsworth said. "I would say 'Break a leg,' but that might not be wise, so I'll just say good luck."

And after he'd gone, I said to Jared, "What did you mean, it'll probably be me who wins?"

"Well won't it?" he asked. "It usually is."

"Whatever," I said.

34 NERDSTROM IS STUFFED

That Wednesday me and Nerdstrom went to the library as usual. And even though he'd been talking to me a lot more lately, that Wednesday he was back to his shy self. He was reading another one of his big, chunky books, but he seemed kind of distracted.

"What's wrong with you?" I asked him. "You're all like mopey."

"Just do your math," he said.

"But what's wrong?"

"It's nothing. I just hate . . . I just hate all this stuff we have to do."

"Like what?"

And he went, "You hate math, don't you? Yeah, well, I hate having to stand up and talk in front of people. Especially when they make fun of you."

"Oh, is *that* it? What are you doing for that stupid assembly thing, anyway?"

And he scratched at a piece of leftover sticky tape on the top of the desk and said, "I don't know."

And I said, "What do you mean, you don't know? It's this Friday!"

"Yeah, okay, I know *that* much."

"So haven't you prepared anything at all?"

And he nodded, staring down at the desk. "Yep, I did have something I was going to do, but I'm not going to do it now."

"What was it?" I asked.

"It was a stupid idea. But now I can't think of anything else." Then he looked up at me, and he seemed kind of suddenly hopeful. "You and Jared are doing something together, aren't you? Maybe I could . . . like . . . no, that's a dumb idea."

I nodded, "Yeah, you know, Jared can be really . . . really kind of . . ."

"Yeah, dumb idea. It's okay. I'll talk to Ulrika. We'll think of something. By Friday." Then he sighed. "I'm in trouble, aren't I?"

"Yup," I said.

CASEY GETS LOST

That Thursday I had a meat pie for lunch, and it was nice. I bought the pie with my own lunch money, just like I usually did, and I ate it with Jared, just like I usually did. We ate our lunch quickly, because we wanted to practice the words of our routine again, since the big performance was the next day.

Casey came over. He didn't have his whole posse with him this time. In fact he was all by himself, and I said, "Hey, Casey, where's the rest of your gang?"

And Casey said, "They're with Dallas Lindsay."

"Who's Dallas Lindsay?"

"He's just this guy from third grade. They said that they want to hang around with him today."

"Can't you hang around with him too?" I asked.

But Casey shook his head. "He doesn't like me. So can I stay with you guys for a while?"

"No," said Jared. "No, you can't. We've got to practice our thing for tomorrow."

"Can't I watch you practice? I can help you re-member your words and stuff."

"No. Go away," said Jared. "In case you didn't know, you're in first grade, and we're in sixth grade. And I know you've got a brother in high school, but that's too bad. Go away. We're busy doing big kid stuff, so get lost."

Then Casey looked at me, as if I could say it was okay for him to stay. But I didn't know what to do, so I just said, "You know what? Maybe we'll see you later, Casey, all right? You should go and find some other kids your own age to play with. Go on. I'll talk to you later."

"But no one wants to play with me. They all hate me," said Casey.

And I felt sad for him, which was a weird kind of feeling, but I said, "We've got stuff to do, mate, so I'll see you later on."

"Okay. Bye," said Casey.

And as he turned and walked away, I heard Jared say, in just a mutter, really, "Yeah, get lost, you wannabe."

I think Casey might have been crying but I hadn't planned for that. I wasn't trying to make him cry. Honest.

36 WE HAVE OUR STUPID BOOK ASSEMBLY

That Friday we had our Literature Day assembly, and our class had to sit in the front two rows of the hall. Some of the kids had come dressed up ready to do skits, with costumes and everything. Hayley Belgrado and all her revolting plastic girlfriends had come as the cast of one of those teenage soapy shows, which I think probably made Mr. Sigsworth a little cranky, since he'd told us all about a million times that our material had to be taken from books, not TV shows or movies.

And Bunty Grierson was wearing a Little Bo Peep outfit, and several of her posse had dressed as sheep, which seemed like a pretty lame option, really, unless she was going to hold them down and shear them. A couple of the boys had come in cammo gear and black face paint, and I reckoned they were going to do some famous wartime speech from some book about bomber pilots. And Claudio di Marco had

185

a guinea pig in a box, and when we asked him who he was, he said he was Do-wrong Ron, whoever *that* is.

And of course me and Jared were wrestlers. We'd made sure that we'd chosen wrestlers who always wear T-shirts and jeans, so we wouldn't have to think too hard about our costumes.

Just before assembly was due to start, Jared said to me, "Where's Nerdstrom? I haven't seen him."

"Me either."

"Maybe he's gone all chicken, as usual."

"Maybe."

"Maybe he's coming as the chicken from that movie. Or maybe he's just putting on his *Star Wars* costume."

"It's got to be out of a book, you idiot," I said. "And anyway, he doesn't even like *Star Wars*."

"Well, excuse me," Jared said.

And then Nerdstrom appeared, standing in the doorway of the hall.

"Who's *he* come as—King Arthur?" I heard someone behind me say.

Jared cracked up, and so did I, but maybe not as much as Jared. Nerdstrom was wearing a long shirt-thing that looked like it had been made out of an old sack, and he had a wide belt around his waist. Plus he was carrying a large cardboard shield and a sword made out of something that obviously wasn't metal, and on his head he had a slightly misshapen papier-mâché knight's helmet that had been spray-painted silver. As he got inside the hall he dragged the helmet off his head and held it at his side. I could almost feel the glow of the heat from his red face.

Nerdstrom slunk closer and sat down at the end of the row, next to Vinod Rashan, who was dressed as a

hobbit, I think. It looked like Nerdstrom was counting the floorboards at his feet as he stared straight down, and his lips were moving slightly.

"It's Sir Triffin the Bashful," I said.

And Jared said, "Yeah, Sir Triffin the Bashful, Earl of Papier-Mâché."

"Careful—he might turn you into a piñata," said Tom Edwards, who was sitting behind us, and we cracked up some more.

"I bet Ulrika helped him with that," I said.

"Who?" asked Jared. "Who's Ulrika?"

"No one," I said.

"Dude, who's Ulrika?"

And I felt my heart kind of sinking down in my

chest, because I knew he wouldn't stop until he knew the truth. *All* of the truth. "That's his mum," I said. "Nerdstrom's mum is called Ulrika."

Casey's first grade class came in then, all walking in a double row and holding hands, led by their teacher, Miss Hopkins. They walked right across in front of where we were sitting, and as Casey went past he held out his hand for me and Jared to give him a high-five. I did, but Jared wouldn't. He just kept his hands in his lap and looked at me through these squinty eyes.

"What's up *your* nose?" I asked him.

He shook his head. "Nothing. I just don't like that kid anymore."

"Well, I still do. I reckon he's pretty cool," I said.

"Whatever."

Then Mr. Sigsworth was at the front, tapping his finger against the microphone. The speakers went pop and thump, and gradually the kids in the audience started to quiet down. "Thanks, everyone, if we can settle down for a minute . . . Thank you . . . I'm still waiting for you, Ms. Finch's class. Good, thank you. All right, today my sixth grade class will be taking assembly for us, and they'll be presenting excerpts from books that they have enjoyed." Then he looked at Hayley Belgrado and her friends and said, "At least, *most* are from books. Anyway, let's get started with Gladys Mulholland, who'll be acting out her favorite scene from *Charlie and the Chocolate Factory.*"

Most of us hadn't seen the other acts, and some of them were pretty good, except for Hayley and her friends who just walked around on the stage pretending to text each other, saying things like, "Oh my gosh that is so awesome" and "Isn't he like totally *hot?*" until I felt like screaming.

Then there was Marla Mackenzie and Eva Thoung who did some long and boring speech by Shakespeare, full of *thees* and *thines* and other words that no one ever uses anymore, and eventually Mr. Sigsworth had to stand up and quietly ask them to finish, which

they finally did. And they gave this big bow, even though hardly anyone was clapping, and those that were probably clapped because it was finally over.

And then it was me and Jared's turn, and even though we'd practiced heaps, it felt kind of weird as we stood up there. I could see all the kids in their rows, with the little ones near the front, all the way back to the other sixth grade classes. I spotted Casey a couple of rows back and he waved, but I ignored him. I was in the zone, ready to perform, more or less.

I went up to the microphone and said, "Hi, everyone, we looked at this book," and I held up the library copy of *A Photographic Guide to the World of Professional Wrestling* so everyone could see it. Then I said, "Today I'm going to be Bobby Bloodhound, and Jared *was* going to be Nemesis, but we couldn't find any gold face paint, so he's going to be Jake Typhoon instead." And most of the boys in the hall cheered, especially the little ones. Especially Casey, I noticed.

Then I stepped back from the mike, turned to Jared, and pointing right at his face, I shouted, "Typhoon, you have come here tonight expecting to take the world championship belt home with you, but you are wrong, my friend, you are so *wrong!*"

And Jared bellowed, "I ain't no friend of yours, Bloodhound, so you can take that attitude and put it well out of sight, if you get my meanin'! I ain't never backing down, I ain't never givin' in, and I sure ain't goin' home without no belt, you *hear* me?"

And I shouted, "Oh yeah?"

Then he shouted, "Oh *yeah!*"

And the whole time the kids in the audience were starting to scream louder and louder, and they wouldn't have been able to hear anything we were saying to each other anyway, so it was just as well that the next part of our act was the physical bit.

I grabbed Jared by the front of his shirt and threw him down onto the stage, and there was this huge thump as he hit the floor. And even though he knew in advance that I was going to throw him down, because we'd practiced it, he still looked a tiny bit surprised, and he made this little sound that sounded like I'd punched him in the back, right between the shoulder blades.

Then he was rolling on top of me, and pretending to hit me while he slapped the floor at the same time, and then I jumped up and got behind him and put a stranglehold on him. He tried to pretend-punch me in the face by swinging his arm behind him, but he

didn't miss like he was meant to, but got me right in the lip, which really hurt. And the kids in the audience loved it, as I grabbed at my lip and saw some blood.

"What do you think you're doing?" I asked.

But Jared was standing there with his fists clenched, and he had this snarl on his face that I'd never seen before. It was weird, seeing that face he was making, because I've seen Jared angry and mean before, but this time it was way angrier and way, *way* meaner.

"What do I think I'm doing?" he hissed. "I'm just being a wrestler. What are *you* doing?" And he kind of leapt at me. I moved out of the way just in time, but his elbow bounced off my ear, which made it really sting.

The kids were screaming big-time as I turned and saw that Jared was off balance. I hit him with my shoulder, right in the chest, and he sort of went "Oof" and fell down. That was when I put a hammer-drop on him, but I didn't try very hard to hit the floor first like you're supposed to, and I heard him go "Oof" again. I grabbed one of his ears then and started to twist it, and I think I heard him squeal. And that felt good, actually, hearing Jared squeal, because I'd only ever seen him make other people squeal.

Then Mr. Sigsworth was pulling me off Jared, and then he was sort of standing between us, and he was going, "Okay, thanks boys, that was fantastic. Boys? Boys! *Boys!*" And by then he'd actually pulled us apart, and when I looked at Jared he was puffing hard, and he seemed properly angry, and his fists were still clenched, and his ear was all red. Then I glanced down at my own fists and saw that they were clenched too. And when I wiped my mouth with the back of my hand, it came away smeared with blood.

"Not quite what I meant by settling it to the death, guys," Mr. Sigsworth said to us. "Off you go. Go and sit down now." Then he said into the microphone,

"Thanks, boys. That was a realistically graphic portrayal of the most dramatic chapter in . . . in whatever book you were working from. Mrs. Booth, would you mind getting Max a tissue . . . thanks, Mrs. Booth. Wow, that was more intense than it was in practice."

We went and sat down, and I pressed it against my lip, which was stinging and felt kind of fat. But me and Jared didn't look at each other, and I thought that maybe we'd have to talk afterwards and try to kind of work out what had happened, and how playing at being wrestlers had turned into me getting a bleeding lip.

Mr. Sigsworth had the microphone again, and he checked the list in his hand, cleared his throat and said, "Now we've got a real treat, because our next performance is from Triffin Nordstrom."

And I heard someone shout, "Nerdstrom!" behind me, and Mr. Sigsworth frowned in their direction. "Thanks, everyone, there's no need for . . . okay, if you can just settle down . . . Triffin? Are you ready?"

And I was thinking how much of a rhetorical question *that* was.

Mr. Sigsworth sat down on his chair at the side of the stage and Nerdstrom stood up slowly at the end of our row and walked toward the steps leading up to the stage. There wasn't much sound from the audience. In fact it was really quiet as he walked up there. And he leaned toward Mr. Sigsworth and whispered something, and Sigsy nodded and came over to the mike again. "Sorry, the next performance is by *Finn* Nordstrom," he said. "Thanks, Finn."

And there was Nerdstrom standing in front of the microphone, with his stupid potato-sack shirt and his cardboard shield and his not-metal sword and his papier-mâché helmet. And he stood there and looked so scared, and didn't say anything for ages.

That was when someone whistled, and a few people giggled, and a couple of the teachers shushed the gigglers.

And Nerdstrom looked across at Mr. Sigsworth, who just nodded once, as if to say, "You're okay."

But he wasn't okay. He was frozen there, like an escaping prisoner caught in a spotlight.

Then some kid shouted, "Get on with it, Finn!" and got shushed as well.

And at last, after what felt like ages, Nerdstrom did get on with it, sort of. He started to talk but his voice didn't work at all. So he cleared his throat and started again. He said, "This is one of my favorite poems. I like it because it's nonsense, but it still makes sense, even though . . . You'll . . . you'll see." He looked toward Mr. Sigsworth again, and then he coughed a couple of times and adjusted his helmet, but it was still crooked, and looking really ridiculous.

"'Jabberwocky,' by Lewis Carroll," he said, and a few kids tittered. Nerdstrom paused, as if he'd forgotten his words. Then he started, and his voice was a little wobbly. "''Twas brillig, and the slithy toves did gyre and gimble in the wabe.'"

A few kids laughed, and when I checked over my shoulder I saw a few raised eyebrows as well, as if the kids were saying to each other, "What is *this?*"

Nerdstrom took a deep breath, and because I was sitting in the front row I heard the breath shudder as he blew it out. "All . . . all mimsy were the borogroves, and the mome raths outgrabe."

Behind me, I heard Tom Edwards muttering, "I'll mimsy your borogroves in a minute, you weedy little dweeb."

And I glanced at Jared, who I expected would be laughing, but he wasn't. He was just having this huge sulk.

It looked like Nerdstrom was stuck again, because there was another one of those long, uncomfortable pauses. Then he quietly repeated the end of the last line, just to get himself going again, I guess. "'And the mome raths outgrabe.'"

"You already said that," I heard some kid say, and Mr. Sigsworth must have heard it as well, because he scowled at the kid like crazy.

Nerdstrom tried to keep going. "'Beware the Jabberwock, my son, the claws that bite . . . sorry, the *jaws* that bite, the claws that catch. Beware the Jubjub bird and shun the frumious Bandersnatch.'"

I felt myself take a deep breath as well. He was still going all right, even though some of the audience was getting fidgety.

But then he was stuck again. He opened his mouth to say the next line, but it didn't come out. "Um . . . sorry. Um . . . 'Beware the Jabberwock, my son' . . . no, I already . . . 'the frumious Bandersnatch' . . . um . . ." Nerdstrom was blinking a lot as he reached up and dragged the helmet off his head. It hung at his side, next to his cardboard shield and his not-metal sword. His face was glowing red-hot by now.

And then something happened. I could hardly believe it, but I heard my own voice calling out, not loudly, but hopefully just loud enough for Nerdstrom to hear. My voice said, "'He took his vorpal sword in hand.'"

Nerdstrom heard me, because his eyes flickered in my direction, and I saw him straighten his shoulders slightly. "'He took his vorpal sword in hand, long time the manxome foe he sought. So rested he . . . so rested he . . .' um . . ."

"'By the Tumtum tree,'" I said.

"'So rested he by the Tumtum tree, and stood awhile in thought . . .'"

But Nerdstrom's memory had dried up again. He stood there, totally silent for ages, while the audience squirmed around and the teachers checked their watches and bit their lips and scratched their foreheads.

"Um . . . ," said Nerdstrom again. His face was the color of a ripe strawberry, and he was swallowing like crazy.

"It's all right," I heard Mr. Sigsworth say quietly.

"What a loser," I heard Jared mumble.

I guess that normally I would have agreed with him, and would have totally enjoyed seeing Nerdstrom look like a jerk. But this time I didn't. This time I did something peculiar and unexpected. I stood up, walked across the floor to the stage, and started to climb the steps.

Nerdstrom looked at me like I was about to do something awful to him. But I stood next to him, and I said, quite loudly and into the microphone, "'And as in uffish thought he stood, the Jabberwock, with eyes of flame, came whiffling through the tulgey wood, and burbled as it came.'"

I heard a swoosh as Nerdstrom drew his not-metal sword from his belt and held it high above his head. He'd found his spot now, and he was away. He said, in a louder voice, "'One two! One two! And through and through, the vorpal blade went snicker-snack.'"

I wondered if I should sit down, but then when I heard his sword swooshing and snicker-snacking in the air around me, I suddenly turned into the Jabberwock, with the jaws that bite and the claws that catch, and as Nerdstrom launched into the next line I knew that I was about to lose my head. I gave a huge, Jabberwockish roar and fell all twitchy onto the stage, while Nerdstrom carried on reciting. "'He left it dead, and with its head he came galumphing back.'"

Nerdstrom didn't need me anymore, but I lay there on the stage anyway as he kept going with his poem. "'And hast thou slain the Jabberwock? Come to my arms, my beamish boy! Oh frabjous day! Callooh! Callay! he chortled in his joy.'"

He was nearly at the end now, and he reached down for my hand, and I took it, and he lifted me up onto my feet. "Together," he said under his breath, and we did the last verse totally together, totally, as if we'd actually practiced it together.

""'Twas brillig, and the slithy toves did gyre and gimble in the wabe. All mimsy were the borogroves, and the mome roths outgrabe.'"

And we bowed.